DANCE OF THE
BANISHED

DANCE OF THE BANISHED

Marsha Forchuk Skrypuch

pajamapress

First published in the United States in 2015

10 9 8 7 6 5 4 3 2 1

www.pajamapress.ca info@pajamapress.ca

The publisher gratefully acknowledges the support of the Canada Council for the Arts and the Ontario Arts Council for its publishing program. We acknowledge the financial support of the Government of Canada through the Canada Book Fund for our publishing activities.

Library and Archives Canada Cataloguing in Publication

Skrypuch, Marsha Forchuk, 1954-, author   Dance of the banished / Marsha Forchuk Skrypuch.

ISBN 978-1-927485-65-1 (pbk.)

I. Title.

PS8587.K79D35 2014   jC813'.54   C2014-903335-4

Publisher Cataloging-in-Publication Data (U.S.)

Skrypuch, Marsha Forchuk, 1954-

   Dance of the banished / Marsha Forchuk Skrypuch.

[240] pages : cm.

Summary: A teenager leaves his fiancé behind in their Anatolian village to make a new life in Canada for them both. But when World War I breaks out, he is sent to an internment camp while his betrothed struggles to survive and find a way to join him.

ISBN-13: 978-1-927485-65-1 (pbk.)

1. Canada – History – 20th century – Juvenile fiction. 2. World War, 1914-1918 – Canada, Internment camps – Juvenile fiction. 3. Canada – Immigration and emigration – Juvenile fiction. I. Title.

[Fic] dc23   PZ7.S5696da 2014

Cover illustration–Pascal Milelli
Map illustration–John Lightfoot
Photographs courtesy of Ron Morel Memorial Museum, Kapuskasing, Ontario
Cover and interior design–Rebecca Buchanan

Manufactured by Friesens.
Printed in Canada.

Pajama Press Inc.
181 Carlaw Ave. Suite 207, Toronto, Ontario Canada, M4M 2S1

Distributed in Canada by UTP Distribution
5201 Dufferin Street Toronto, Ontario Canada, M3H 5T8

Distributed in the U.S. by Orca Book Publishers
PO Box 468 Custer, WA, 98240-0468, USA

For the forgotten ones

Prologue

Eyolmez, Anatolia
June 1, 1913

Zeynep stood before me, her head tilted in concern. "What's the matter?"

I hesitated as I stared at the dimple on Zeynep's cheek, at her messy hair tied loosely in a piece of red silk. The thought of leaving her was almost more than I could bear.

"You know that Hagop Gregorian's taking my brother with him when he travels back to Canada tomorrow. Well, it won't just be Yousef going; Hagop is taking me too."

She gasped.

"Hagop's nephew Krikor was supposed to go, but you know he is sick," I said quickly. "It would have been a waste of an expensive ticket if someone didn't fill his place. Mama convinced Hagop to take me instead."

A wave of anger passed over Zeynep's face. "You promised we'd go together."

"How many years would it take us to save up for two tickets?" I asked. "Mama convinced Hagop to *give* me this ticket. Now I can go, take the job Hagop found for Krikor, and earn enough money for Mama's taxes and your ticket. It will be faster this way."

"But it's not—," began Zeynep. Then she stopped. She knew I was right. No one bought our rugs or silk anymore. Our mountain pastures and patchy fields produced barely enough to feed us. It was impossible to make money here. The only people getting fat were the tax collectors.

The men took turns working in another country for a few years—sometimes even decades—and sent their earnings home. The women could then pay the taxes and buy food for the children, but it was a lonely existence for everyone. When the men came back years later, sometimes they didn't recognize their own family. Some of the men never returned. That's why Zeynep and I had decided to leave for Canada together. But for all our planning, we hadn't managed to save any money.

Suddenly, with Krikor's illness, everything changed. Hagop had a rooming house in Canada. There was a good foundry job waiting for me. The freedom that loomed in front of me both frightened and excited me. Why couldn't Zeynep be happy for me—for us?

"We may have nicer houses, but with the men all gone, the heart of this village is dead," said Zeynep.

"I'll come back for you as soon as I save the money. We'll get married. In the meantime, I've brought you a gift." I reached into my bag and drew out two identical journals. "One of these is for you. While we are apart, keep this journal for me and I'll write in the other for you. As you fill each page, tear it out and mail it to me. I'll do the same. That way, we will still be together."

Zeynep took the journal and frowned, flipping through its blank pages. "I refuse to be your betrothed, never knowing when, or even if, you'll come back."

She pulled a thin leather strap from around her neck. Strung on it was her cherished blue evil-eye bead that had protected her ever since she was a baby. "Take this." She stood on her tiptoes to put it over my head. "It will keep you from harm. I'll always love you, but I will not wait for you. We both deserve better than that."

She turned and walked away.

Zeynep's betrayal shook me to the core. How would I live with the other half of me gone?

PART ONE

Chapter One

EYOLMEZ, ANATOLIA

June 5, 1913

Dear Ali,

When I placed my cherished evil-eye pendant around your neck for good luck, I meant it when I said that I loved you. But just because I love you, it doesn't mean that I will wait for you. I am writing in this book like you told me to, but I won't tear a page out of it and mail it to you until I receive a letter from you first.

Did you forget the promise you made to me when we were children? Didn't we cut our palms with the same knife, mingle our blood together, and pledge to love each other above all else?

We were supposed to escape together.

I don't believe you when you say that you'll write. Now that you have left, you've put me out of your mind. That's what the men do when they leave. We aren't likely to ever meet again. I don't believe it when you say that you'll come back.

But if you do return, maybe I'll show you this journal, and then you'll know how badly I've been hurt.

Yes, you have a duty to your mother, but as I stood beside her today and we waved our last good-bye, you couldn't miss that satisfied smirk of hers. Don't fool yourself, Ali. She planned your early departure down to the last minute. She has never liked me.

The wives are the wealthy ones, with their shiny bangles and new scarves—bought with the sweat of their absent men. They plod along on their thick ankles with their heads held high. They think they're better than I am. But I've seen the worry lines where there used to be smiles. They may have money from their husbands across the sea, but that is all.

You wanted a promise of marriage before you left, and your eyes turned to stone when I said no. I love you, Ali, but I will never sit around and wait while life passes me by.

It is a few days later. At least now the weather is warm and I can go up to the mountains with the younger women and children. That little cottage near where our sheep and goats graze—it is my favorite place in the world. I love to watch the spring lambs as they balance on their hind legs and nibble the new shoots on bushes. I love to stand on top of our special rock and drink in the universe. The blue sky and snowcapped mountains seem close enough for me to touch. The meadow rolls out below me like a carpet of grass, rocks, and wildflowers. When I am up here I can believe what the dede preaches, that God is inside all of us, and God is the universe. Remember when you came with me to the mountains and you held me all through the night as we sat on this very rock? My heart aches with longing. Why did you have to leave?

It's crowded inside the mountain cottage at night, so I take my bedding up to the roof and sleep under the moon and stars. Is it the same moon where you are, Ali? When you look up at the night sky, do you think of me?

August 7, 1913

It is still warm during the day in the mountains, but the nights are getting too cold to sleep outside. There's no advantage to staying up here because the cottage is just as crowded as our house. Mama needs help with the cheese making, so now I've come back home. All this time I've been gone and no letter from you. I refuse to be disappointed. It's up to me to make my own future.

Being back in the village has steeled my resolve to leave. The dede says that women and men are equal, but when I look at the women in our village I cannot agree. How can a woman be equal to a man when it's the women who have the babies and nurture them? Yes, we Alevi women can walk unveiled and we worship beside our men; but until someone else has the babies, we will never be equal. You should see my cousin Fatma now. She was the most promising student in the missionary school, but now she's big with child again. Your brother Yousef was only home for a few months. Will he ever be able to afford to stay home permanently if Fatma gets pregnant the moment he steps through the door?

September 5, 1913

Ali, your mother is not a kind woman. I know you love her—it's your duty. But she's complained to the dede, telling him that I don't belong here anymore. All I did was point out to Cousin Fatma that she could do something more with her life than have babies. I didn't say it in an unkind way. We were chatting together at the well and she lorded it over me with her giant belly and the new gold earrings she'd bought from the money Yousef had sent her. That made me so angry! If she'd just save her money and stop having babies, he'd be able to come home sooner. She also told me that she's received three letters from Yousef since he's left. She asked sweetly how many I had received from you. Now that I think of it, perhaps I expressed my opinion in a loud voice, but I didn't say it to hurt her feelings.

Why did your mother have to get involved? This was between Fatma and me—a private conversation between cousins—although

I did notice that several of the other women stopped gossiping and leaned in to hear us. Then they whispered to each other, pointing at me, blaming me. And for what? Stating the truth?

We would have settled the argument ourselves. I would have forgiven Fatma for her unkind remarks. But your mother stepped in, put her arm around Fatma, and handed her a cloth to dry her tears. Your mother looked at me with those fierce eyes and said, "You are disrupting our community."

I don't know what she means by that. I work as hard as anyone, and I'm smarter than most, but I am always judged. Why did you leave me, Ali? I am shriveling up inside.

During the discussion before prayers, as the entire community sat together, your mother asked the dede how she was to deal with me. Ali, what I do is none of your mother's business. You left me. We are no longer betrothed. Why can't your mother accept that?

How embarrassing it was to sit there and listen to the elders discuss me as if I were an object, a possession. When the time came to say the prayers, the dede placed his hand over mine and stared at me with his rheumy eyes. "Open your soul to God, my daughter. Your path to truth is yet to be revealed."

What did he mean by that?

Dancing the ritual semah was strange without you, Ali. My brother Turabi partnered me. Fatma's brother Hassan danced with your mother and Riza danced with mine. I closed my eyes and chanted the prayer as we stepped and twirled, and I dreamed of you.

November 13, 1913

Fatma gave birth last night. For all the fuss the women around her made you'd think she'd achieved an impossible feat. Her little daughter has a scrunched-up face and a long tuft of black hair on her forehead, just like her big brother Suleyman did when he was born. You should hear how this baby screams. Fatma smiled at me when I held a glass of honey tea to her lips. "I think I'll name her Zeynep," she said. "She expresses her opinions as freely as you do."

Now that Fatma has a son and a daughter, I hope she'll restrain herself when Yousef next comes home. It would be nice if they could save some money for a change.

December 12, 1913

I can hardly believe that I'm saying this, but maybe your mother was right to make you leave when you did. The army took Turabi, Riza, and Hassan. From the Armenian Quarter, Krikor and Shant were taken. Our Alevi boys may be treated slightly better than the Armenians because at least we're not Christian like they are. But oh, Ali, Turabi is too young to die. I am so worried about him. If you were still here, you would have been rounded up as well.

When I pass your mother by the well, her eyes pierce me. At least she doesn't say out loud what I know she's thinking, that I am a stupid selfish girl who doesn't know what's best for her or her son. I do agree with her about one thing—I don't belong here. I have to get away. You made your escape and you left me behind. It's time for me to figure out my own escape.

March 3, 1914

The village is abuzz with news of our American visitors. Two women and a man—Protestant missionaries. They have inspected our school and are trying to convert us. The Armenians are already Christian, so the missionaries have taken up residence in that part of the village, in the Widow Hartunian's inn.

When Mama was a young bride, the first group of Protestant missionaries arrived, making it possible for our men to find work in North America. I should be angry with them. They disrupted our lives, creating absent men and abandoned wives. Mama disagrees. She says that before the missionaries came and opened the pathway to the West, our village was dying. Is it alive now? In Mama's eyes, it is.

We had all been invited to meet the missionaries. I put on my clean blouse and wrapped my braid in red silk, then walked with Mama down to the Armenian Quarter. Widow Hartunian's gates were wide open. Wooden benches had been placed on the grass and villagers—both Alevi and Christian—were taking their places. Mama and I sat down on the first bench.

The missionaries strode in. They had windburned faces, and

the women, who sat down in chairs facing us, were dressed in gray. The yellow-haired man walked over to a wooden podium. At first he didn't say a word. He just regarded us patiently through wire-framed spectacles that magnified his watery blue eyes. We all fell silent. And then he began to speak—not in English, but in Armenian. He spoke with a funny twist on the endings of his words, but his voice boomed with authority. Listening to him was like being transfixed by the evil eye. I have no idea what he said, because much of it made no sense. He kept talking about how we should come to Jesus, as if Jesus were a person walking the earth right now. I turned around and looked at the audience. Many of the Armenians were nodding, but the dede sat with his arms crossed in anger. Fatma had fallen asleep with baby Zeynep clasped in her arms. Your mother sat just behind Fatma, and when I caught her eye, she gave me a small, cold smile.

The man finally sat down. One of the women got up to the podium. Her hair was pulled back tightly from her face and tied into a knot behind her head in a most unattractive way. Her hair, dress, and hands were all shades of gray. Only her cheeks had color. Her voice didn't boom, so I was glad that I had chosen to sit so close. I bent forward to hear. She talked about a hospital in Harput, where she worked. Poor people would come to the hospital and she would cure them of their illnesses. She gave examples of those she'd helped—blind people and lepers and those near death with typhoid fever. She did all this to honor her God, Jesus. It seemed hard to believe that this woman could be so powerful, but no one contradicted her.

I watched her mouth move as she spoke of these wondrous things, and I longed to be her.

What would it be like to see the mighty city of Harput with my own eyes? I had heard about this huge place high on a hill that overlooked the plains of Anatolia. There were schools there, and hospitals, and people from all over the world. Maybe I couldn't get to Canada right now, but could I reach Harput? At least it would be away from here.

When the healer sat down, the other woman stood. Like the man, she wore wire-framed glasses, but hers didn't make her eyes look unnaturally large. Her black hair was loosely braided and fastened with a red ribbon. It hung long over one shoulder, just the way I wear my own. In fact, I imagined myself standing up there, with everyone hanging on my every word. Unlike the two other missionaries, this woman didn't preach. She looked at people in the audience, as if searching for someone she knew. Her eyes rested on me, and she asked, in perfectly pronounced Armenian, "Do you like to read?"

I was so shocked that I just sat there, my mouth hanging open. Mama elbowed me, jolting me out of my stupor.

"Answer her," she hissed.

"I like to read," I said.

The woman smiled. She looked around. "Anyone else here who likes to read?"

A few hands went up.

It was an odd question, and it made me a bit angry. Who doesn't like to read? It's the way you find out information. It's also the way for your imagination to leave home even if your body is trapped. But the problem is that there is nothing for us to read. Newspapers arrive infrequently, and we have no books. Some people get letters from America, but I don't.

But once she began to explain, I understood. This woman, who told us her name was Miss Anton, was a teacher. "I have a school for orphans in Harput," she said. "My children learn to read and write, and they're taught a craft. We have saved many children from hunger and death. They are now productive citizens." My heart pounded with excitement as I listened to her, Ali. I wanted to be Miss Anton even more than I wanted to be the healing woman.

After the missionaries finished speaking, I waited in line for a chance to speak to Miss Anton. "I want to work at your school," I told her.

She smiled. "Are you a Christian?

"I'm an Alevi Kurd."

"Are you willing to become a Christian?" she asked.

"Alevis believe in Jesus, the sun, the moon, the stars, and Allah. Doesn't that mean we're already Christian?"

Her face went slack with my pronouncement. "Certainly not. To become a Christian, you'd have to give up those false gods."

I was about to ask her more, but she turned away from me to speak with someone else.

March 6, 1914

The missionaries stayed for a few days and I kept track of them as best I could. I especially wanted to learn more about Miss Anton, but whenever she saw me, she'd look the other way. For someone who was supposed to be turning people into Christians, you'd think that she'd try a little bit harder with me.

One day I confronted her as she sipped tea in Petrosian's shop in the Armenian Quarter. "I want to come to Harput," I said, "to be your helper."

She set her cup down with a clatter and sighed. "No, you cannot come with me. That's final. If I took in every young girl with romantic ideas of becoming a missionary, I'd never get any work done." She fumbled through her satchel and pulled out a coin. Setting it on the table, she rose and strode out of the store.

If she won't allow me to go with her, I'll have to take matters into my own hands.

March 10, 1914

That night, I tucked my journal into my second set of clothing and tied my kerchief around everything. I kissed Mama's cheek and slipped a note under her pillow. Then I tiptoed out of our house. When men leave the village, all the women, children, and old people stand in a line and wave tearfully. But when I left, no one even knew. As I passed your mother's house, I saw a silhouette at the window. Was it your mother watching me leave? Would she wish me good luck? Or would her lips curve upward as she rejoiced?

I waited at our village gates for the missionaries to pass. Just as the sun rose, I heard the *clip-clop* of their horse-drawn wagon. I hid behind a tree until they passed, and then I stepped in behind them.

The wagon didn't appear to be going very fast, but I had to trot to keep up, and my handmade boots were not made for trotting—especially on a frozen, rutted road. I slipped and fell more than once and was soon covered with icy mud, but I avoided twisting an ankle. I nearly lost everything when the kerchief became untied and all my worldly goods spilled out onto the road. I wasted precious minutes packing the muddy items back into my scarf, and I panicked as I saw the wagon move farther and farther away. I could have wept with relief when the missionaries finally made a brief stop midmorning to stretch their legs and feed the horses. It gave me a chance to catch up, but I was so exhausted I knew that I couldn't go on. I hid behind a bush, and just as the wagon began to move again, I grabbed onto the back ledge and pulled myself up. The wagon bed was covered with canvas but it was a flat load, so I had to crouch down at an awkward angle whenever one of the missionaries turned around.

As I held on for dear life, my fingers nearly froze. It's not easy to stay hidden while balancing on a thin ledge of wood on a wagon that is sliding over sheets of ice and bouncing into muddy sinkholes. While traveling in this uncomfortable fashion, I thought of you. Every step of your journey away from me had been planned and paid for. You didn't have to clutch onto the back of a wagon to get away. And when you arrived at your destination, there was a place waiting for you. I'm not blaming you, Ali, and I'm not really angry anymore. I just wish life were a bit fairer.

After an hour or so, one of the women let out a shrill scream. The wagon halted so suddenly that I nearly lost my balance. I was so worried about what had frightened her that I began to fret. What if it were a wild animal, or maybe an armed bandit? I was probably in more danger than they were, since I was hanging precariously onto the end of the wagon. But I had no choice. I let go of the wagon and dropped down into the mud, so they wouldn't see me.

I heard footsteps, and then someone stopped beside me. I looked up.

"It's you." Miss Anton's brow was furrowed as she towered over me, her gloved hands on her hips.

I stood up and attempted to brush off the worst of the mud, but it was no use. If she thought I was unworthy before, my current appearance wouldn't do much to change her mind. The other woman and the man got down from the wagon and stood beside her. The man's blue eyes widened with surprise. The gray-haired woman began to laugh.

"Thank goodness," she said. "It's just a girl. I thought you were a madman come to attack us."

The man reached down and pulled my bundle out of the

mud. "If you wanted to come to Harput with us, why didn't you just ask?"

Before I could say a word, Miss Anton answered. "She did ask, and I told her no."

A tumble of emotions seemed to flash over the man's face before his features settled into a calm expression. "Well, I guess she's coming with us now, Christine."

He held out his hand to me, "I'm Reverend John Emmonds," he said.

The other woman took my muddy fingers in hers and grinned. "I'm his wife, Lenore."

Lenore took me behind a bush and helped brush off all that mud, then she held my dirty clothing as I changed into my second set of clothing, which was dryer and not so muddy. My face was hot with shame as I changed in front of this stranger, but she gazed above my head at the mountains, pretending she didn't see me. "Why did you want to get away so badly?" she asked as I pulled on my second wool vest.

"I want to be like you."

She smiled. "You want to bring the word of Jesus to savages?"

Her question was so ignorant that I didn't know where to begin. Alevi Kurds are not savages, and we do not need a lesson in religion from outsiders. But I was her guest and she was being kind. I chose my words carefully.

"I want to help people who are less fortunate."

"Very good," she said. "I shall find something for you to do at the hospital, if you'd like."

Lenore stored my dirty bundle in the back of the wagon, pulled out a clean warm coat from her own baggage, and insisted I wear it. There was barely room for the four of us on the wagon seat, and Miss Anton refused to sit beside me, so she sat at one end and I sat at the other, with the Emmonds between us. We traveled for the rest of the day squished like this until we reached an inn.

The man came out to meet us and at first he told us that we couldn't stay. I could tell from his expression that he wasn't fond of people like the missionaries. But he was an Alevi Kurd, like I was, and in this area we are all distantly related.

"Uncle," I said in Zaza. "These people are my friends. Surely you could find a spot for us? We'll be gone by sunrise."

He quizzed me about my grandfather and great-grandfather. Once he figured out that we were indeed related, his face broke out in a grin. "Dear Zeynep," he said. "You and your friends are welcome to stay as long as you like."

As we crowded onto the wagon seat the next day, Miss Anton was almost civil to me. They had been used to sleeping outside even in the nastiest weather because the innkeepers weren't friendly to them. She must have realized that I could be useful. I sat quietly and listened to the conversation between the three missionaries, but I pretended to be intensely interested in the muddy fields and snowy mountains. Not all of what they said made sense. A missionaries' convention? Something the matter with a car engine? The dilemma of a lost spat? But then they spoke in hushed tones and I had to lean forward to hear what they said. It was about how the Bulgarians, the Serbians, and the Greeks—all of them Christian—had defeated the Muslim Turks, and how a new war was starting up again. Would my brother Turabi be forced to fight? He is neither Muslim nor Christian, yet he'll be stuck in the middle. My heart aches at the thought of him being put into so much danger.

Ali, I am still angry that you left me, but at least you're safe.

On the third day of our journey, Harput became visible in the distance. I had heard about it before, of course, but never in my imagination had I been able to picture anything this size. Harput is built on the side of a mountain, and from a distance you can see hundreds of rooftops, starting at the base and spreading halfway up the face of the mountain. At the top sits a tumbled-down fortress. Reverend Emmonds says it is a castle that was built 500 years ago. He pointed to a cluster of large buildings partway up the mountain and called it the American College, our destination.

Before we arrived in Harput, we came to another city that also seemed huge, although Lenore says that Harput is much bigger. This city is called Mezreh. As we rode through the streets, we passed a very large house that could barely be seen above tall walls that surrounded it. Lenore said that this is the American Consulate, which is an American government building. Soldiers stood before the front gates, and one of them nodded slightly as our cart passed. They must have recognized the missionaries.

As we made our way through Mezreh, Lenore told me that although Harput is mostly populated by Muslim Turks, Mezreh is half Armenian. It's an important city because it houses the headquarters for the Ottoman Army, and the vali—or governor—for the entire area lives there as well. We passed such a variety of people in the streets—some in flowing wool and silk robes like my own, others wearing traditional clothing except for their store-bought shoes. The Armenians were easy to spot because they were dressed in western clothing like the missionaries. The Turkish women were also easy to identify because they were covered from head to toe in their dark chadors.

The final three miles to Harput were up a steep road and I felt sorry for the horses. When we reached the top, I stepped down from the wagon and looked around. From where I stood, I could see the entire Anatolian plain and could count hundreds of villages, some with just a few houses and others quite large. It's too early in the year for there to be much color, so right now it looks drab and muddy, but in a few weeks the entire plain will burst into color. I can hardly wait to see what that looks like from up here. Lenore says that the villages are mostly Armenian, but wherever there are Armenians, you can find Alevis. She also says that the Euphrates River is just six miles from here, but I couldn't see it. I could see all the way to the Dersim Mountains though, and they're beyond our own mountains. On the other side of the Dersim Mountains is Russia.

To stretch my legs I walked beside the wagon, which moved slowly through the streets. The missionaries stopped at one of the houses, and Miss Anton climbed down from the wagon. She pulled her luggage from the back. "It was a successful trip," she said, looking at the minister and his wife. "I'll see you tomorrow." She went inside without saying a word to me.

The reverend and Lenore drove on for a few more minutes before stopping. "This is our house," said the reverend. I wasn't sure what to do. Was I supposed to go inside with them? I helped them with their own luggage, but left mine in the wagon. If need be, I could sleep with the horses. But then Reverend Emmonds grabbed my bundle and carried it in with the rest.

"Our home is simple," he said. "But you are our guest, and what's ours is yours."

Chapter Two

HARPUT, ANATOLIA

April 15, 1914

Ali, these missionaries have very strange customs. While we were traveling, they slept the normal way—everyone snuggled together under the quilt around the warmth of the brazier. But I've looked in every room in the Emmonds' house and there is no place to sleep together. For some reason they've built this house with many rooms, and for much of the time all the rooms are empty. Lenore spends many hours at the hospital and Reverend Emmonds visits people all day and into the evening. There are separate rooms for each person to sleep in, and one room is used for eating only when company comes. There is a separate room for cooking, and there's a table in that room for everyday eating.

When I first arrived, Lenore showed me a room she called "my bedroom." In it stood a bed, which is a sort of sleeping area that is raised off the ground by a metal frame. It has a cushion and several blankets. But it is so cold, sleeping all alone, without a brazier to warm my feet. And it's so quiet, with me being the only person in there.

The only time I've slept by myself is in the summer when I sleep on the roof of our mountain cottage. Whenever I was there, it felt like I was on the top of the world, with just the moon and stars above me. Will I ever go back there? The thought of never returning makes my heart ache. In this bedroom I feel like I am boxed in, but I am determined to get used to it.

My bedroom also has a storage cabinet for clothing. Lenore doesn't think my silk dress and embroidered wool tunic are good for working in the hospital or even for meeting her guests. I think she wants to make me look more like a Christian. She has given me some of her old blouses and skirts, which were too large. Keghani, an Armenian girl who also lives here, showed me how to tighten the seams and move the buttons and clips. Keghani is about my age and she seems friendly. She is from a community not far from ours, so we have no trouble understanding each other. Having her as a friend will help me get over my homesickness.

The missionaries wash in tubs like we do, and of course they have a whole room just for that purpose. Each person in the house has a scheduled weekly time to fill the tub with water that is pumped, and then heated on the stove. Their bars of soap are buttery yellow and smell like roses.

All these empty rooms! Only the reverend, Lenore, Keghani, and I live here. If they organized it differently, this place could shelter six or more families.

The reverend and his wife are both gone for most of the day, but an older Armenian woman named Yester comes in before sunrise and looks after the kitchen—buying food at the market, cooking all the meals, washing the dishes. Her husband Onnig feeds and waters the horses and keeps the wagon in good condition. Yester seems to be about the same age as Mama, but Onnig is probably a decade older than that. There is a small vegetable plot out back, and Onnig looks after it. He seems to especially like gardening. I don't understand why they don't just live here. There's so much extra room.

May 24, 1914

Miss Anton came here for lunch after church. When she saw me in the kitchen helping Yester, she said, "You're still here? I thought you would have taken off by now."

I don't know what she means by that. Miss Anton may have a nice face and pretty hair, but she is a most unpleasant person. As I gathered the dirty dishes from the dining room after lunch, I overheard snippets of conversation. Miss Anton was born in Canada, although she is now an American. I wondered if she came from a place close to where you are, Ali.

Later I asked Lenore about Miss Anton. She was born in a city called Toronto. I asked her if that was close to Brantford. She took an atlas off the bookshelf and showed me. The cities are sixty miles apart, such a long distance. But Lenore explained that things are different there. While it would take weeks to travel that distance here, in Canada there is a train that connects many of the cities together. She said it would only take an hour to get from Brantford to Toronto. Can that really be true? I hope the Canadians you meet are nicer than Miss Anton.

June 12, 1914

Lenore says that a new American consul just arrived a week or so ago. He lives in the government building in Mezreh. Yesterday Keghani and I walked to the Mezreh market, so we could go past the American Consulate to see if anything looks different. The guards held their rifles rigidly at attention and they pretended not to notice us. I was able to get only a glimpse through the metal grillwork at the front. The building is three stories tall and there are beautiful mulberry trees abloom in a huge garden.

June 22, 1914

It has been an adjustment to live the way the missionaries do. I have begun work at the hospital under Lenore's supervision.

Most of the time I sweep floors and change the bed linens. Many people come from far away to be treated in this hospital, and the doctors and nurses turn away no one. Keghani works here too, but her job is to make bandages and mend the bedding and hospital gowns. She says that many Armenian young people come to Harput to learn from the missionaries. Even though they don't believe everything the missionaries say, the Armenians don't mind all the preaching. Their religions are close enough.

Keghani and I work at the hospital from early morning until after lunch, and then we sit in on classes at the college. Most of the instruction is in Armenian, so it is easier to understand than English lectures. But I am determined to learn English as well. Keghani takes a sewing class and I am learning to cook the sort of food that missionaries eat.

I am surprised at how well Lenore gets along in Armenian; but she doesn't speak Zaza at all, so when people from the Dersim Mountains arrive, she calls for me to help. When I greet them in Zaza, they look relieved. These mountain people are Alevi Kurds like us, and they live with Armenians like we do. But their Armenians have mostly adopted Alevi ways, so everyone speaks Zaza. And their customs seem older. The women wear high headdresses decorated with coins, which reminds me of my grandmother. The men have thick black moustaches and beards, and their jackets and wide trousers are made from homespun wool.

Some of these people had to walk twelve or more hours

through steep mountain passes to get here. One elder, whose foot was swollen to the size of a melon, made the journey with the help of his grandson and a hand-carved wooden staff. The mountain people never complain, of course, and they are grateful for the treatment the missionaries offer. I tell them to smile and nod if a missionary comes around and reads from a bible.

The reverend and Lenore treat both Keghani and me as if we were their children, which makes me wonder why they didn't have children of their own. They are so kind to us. We eat our meals together, and when they have company, they introduce us and invite us to stay and listen. If Yester comes in with a tray of refreshments, Lenore includes her in the conversation too, so Yester has to stand around and smile for a bit. Most of Lenore's missionary friends are predictable in their conversations, especially when they find out I'm the only one of the household who isn't Christian, so usually when there's company, I take my leave as soon as it's polite to do so.

Keghani and I have skipped class now and then, so we could explore the streets of Harput and Mezreh. My favorite place is the Harput bazaar with its colorful display of silks and carpets, and the heady scent of spices from around the world. I wish the Emmonds paid me. I yearn now and then to buy a bite of baklava or a sip of yogurt. Yester cooks the way the missionaries prefer, although she will make us treats now and then. Missionary food is filling but not very tasty. Sometimes Yester will cook Armenian food, which is almost identical to ours. The first time I tore off a fresh piece of flat bread and put it in my mouth, I nearly wept. I hadn't realized how much I missed home.

Yes, your mother has been horrible to me, and, yes, the old women were intolerable. I was suffocating. After you left, I believed there was nothing there for me. But the village is my heart and soul. Was it right for me to sneak off at night, with just a note to my mother? Some days I long to go back, but I wonder whether I'd be accepted. Once, the longing was so deep that I asked Lenore if she would take me home. She told me that if I still feel that way by the end of the summer, they will make a special trek out to Eyolmez to take me home before the weather turns. This has set my heart at ease. The distance between our village and Harput would not be far for a bird, but to get through the mud and mountains and bandits—I couldn't do it on my own. I'm not as strong or as brave as the Dersim Mountain people.

Being here in Harput makes me feel like I'm closer to you, Ali. You live among the North Americans. You probably eat their food and wear their clothing. And now I do those things as well. Sometimes at night, I get out of my bed and open my window. I lean out as far as I can and look at the moon and stars. I think of you, halfway around the world, and imagine us both looking at the same moon. We may be apart, but we're together in spirit.

I am still angry with you.

But I'm beginning to forgive you.

July 20, 1914

I received a letter from Mama today. She misses me, but she is not angry with me for leaving. In fact, she's hoping that I can get more schooling with the Americans. The village is changing and it's not safe for me to come back. People in army uniforms move through the area, taking food and clothing without paying. Some have even taken over houses and thrown out the people living there. More young men have been forced to join the army, so anyone who can get away is doing it now. Many elders are hiding in the mountains. Her letter is so disturbing. Has the war come to our village? I pray that Mama is safe.

I am sorry, Ali. Mama also told me about your mother's sudden death. Losing a loved one is always hard, even loved ones who are too generous with their opinions.

I've taken a chance and actually mailed a letter to you. I don't know why I bother, since you've never answered the previous ones. But I miss you so much and am willing to forgive just about anything, especially now that you are grieving the death of your mother. Your devotion to her was admirable, Ali, because truly she didn't deserve it. What I don't understand is how you devoted yourself to your mother even when she was being unreasonable, yet you gave up so soon on me.

I almost forgot—bundled inside the letter from Mama was one from Fatma. Since your mother died, she had been living alone in the house with four-year-old Suleyman and Baby Zeynep. Aunt Besee, Fatma's mother, has moved in to keep her company. Aunt Besee has been so sad and lonely since the army took her son Hassan. Fatma has sorted through your mother's things and put them away for safekeeping, so the children won't ruin them: her gold-coin wedding headdress, a small Chinese enameled lap table for writing letters, and those ruby earrings from Russia. She told me a strange thing, Ali. She says she owes me an apology. I don't know why. Fatma says if we ever see each other again, she will explain in person. I wonder what is on her mind?

Baby Zeynep is six months old now. It's hard to believe. Suleyman loves his sister so much. He tries to feed her from his own plate—nuts and figs and things. Fatma has to watch him because the baby could choke.

Fatma says they've spent much of the summer in the mountains with the sheep and that she misses me. For all the harsh words I've had for cousin Fatma in the past, I must admit that I miss her too. I dreamed that she came here to be with me and that she lived in this bedroom with me. Isn't that a funny idea? But really, Ali, this bedroom is the same size as our entire house in Eyolmez. There's room for them all.

I wrote her back and let her know that I love her dearly and wish her well, and that I forgive her for whatever she thinks she needs to apologize for.

July 29, 1914

Missionaries from all over the Ottoman Empire have arrived at the American College for a conference. Many sunburned white people speaking English—so many women holding parasols and wearing long skirts and complicated hats, men in black wool suits that make them sweat and straw hats that don't keep out the sun. Is this what people look like in Canada, Ali? Do you also wear a black suit in the heat? How do you stand it? My high-buttoned blouse and long heavy skirt seem very impractical in July. I've tried to convince Lenore that loose flowing clothes like those we wear in the village would make more sense in any weather, but she doesn't believe me.

Lenore has been entertaining the women missionaries at the house, and Miss Anton has been here nearly every day, annoying us. Keghani and I have not been to the hospital since all the ladies arrived. We assist at home, helping out Yester in the kitchen by cutting cucumber sandwiches into small white squares and circles, and by squeezing lemons for countless pitchers of cold lemonade.

Have you ever been swimming, Ali? I wonder if I've been the one to experience it first. Lenore organized wagons to take the missionary ladies down to Lake Goljuk. It is six miles away from Harput, but we traveled by wagon, so it didn't take as long as you'd think. Yester and Onnig came with us, along with some of their friends. They dug a pit and built a fire underground, then lowered in a big iron pot containing all the ingredients for a stew. They covered up the fire and it cooked while the ladies swam in the lake.

Lenore found a bathing suit for me to borrow. I told her that I didn't know how to swim, but she insisted I try it on anyway. It used to belong to a missionary who has now gone back to America. When I first held up the suit, I couldn't imagine actually wearing it—it's really not much more than a flimsy undergarment. It has broad horizontal black-and-white stripes and is sleeveless with a low neck. From the knees down my legs are completely bare. Lenore laughed out loud when she saw my expression. "All the women will be wearing them," she said. "Please don't be scandalized. I'm a minister's wife, and I'm wearing one."

The water was icy cold, but it did feel wonderful to walk out into the lake. Some of the ladies were good swimmers and got their heads wet, but I only waded out to where the water was waist deep. After the refreshing dip, the outdoor stew tasted wonderful.

The next day we packed up lunch baskets for some of the more energetic mission ladies, so that they could have a picnic in the ice cave. Lenore told Keghani and me that we could come too. It was a long and hot walk up the mountain with the castle looming above us, but I was curious to see the famous cave. Keghani said that the ice in the cave is supposed to be able to cure sickness. If it really works, maybe they should use it in the hospital.

When Keghani and I reached the top, we had a breathtaking view of the entire city of Harput, the Dersim Mountains, the Euphrates River, and the blue sky all around. Being on top of the world like this reminded me of the summers we spent in our own mountains. My heart ached for you, Ali. I could almost feel the warmth of your arms around me and hear your voice murmuring false promises. Will you ever stop tormenting me?

Keghani and I were faster than the mission ladies, so we arrived at the mouth of the ice cave well before they did. Keghani stepped in first, then I followed her. I stepped through and breathed in deep. The air was so cold. All over the walls, icy water shimmered, and long fingers of ice hung from above. It was a truly magical place, Ali. In the middle of the cave was a narrow hole so deep it just looked black. We settled in a spot far away from the hole. Keghani said that people had fallen through and had disappeared forever.

Chattering noisily, the mission ladies entered the cave, spread out blankets upon the ice, and opened up their baskets. Even in this wonder of a cave, they mostly talked about how to convert the savages to their idea of religion. I know that they mean well, but if they actually took the time to understand what other people believe, they might find that their own ideas aren't superior after all.

Yester had filled our lunch basket with extra treats, so in addition to the tiny cucumber sandwiches and instead of the delicate but tasteless petit fours that the ladies loved, she had slipped in some freshly baked almond cookies. As you know, Mama never made sweets like this at home—we couldn't afford such luxuries—but as I bit into one, again I thought of you. Remember the time you brought me a cookie from Petrosian's?

Keghani was alarmed when she saw the tears in my eyes. She thought I might have cut my tongue on an almond shell, but I stuck it out to show I wasn't hurt.

As we left, I cracked off a long finger of ice from the roof of the cave. Could it really cure sickness? Could it cure a broken heart? I wrapped the cold finger in our towels and nestled it deep within our picnic basket, but when I got home and opened up the basket, there was nothing there.

I almost forgot—we saw the strangest thing when we were up on the mountain today. An American man all by himself, wearing big boots, walking. It wouldn't be strange if it were someone who lived in the mountains, but an American? Lenore looked through her binoculars and smiled. She said it was the new American consul, Leslie Davis. Apparently he is getting quite a reputation for being unusual. Most of the American diplomats who came before him would take half a dozen servants with them wherever they went, and they'd never travel on foot. But Mr. Davis is a simple man. He likes to walk on his own. He calls it "hiking." He takes a camera with him. I wonder if he took a photograph of us?

August 3, 1914

When I arrived at the hospital this morning, the staff was all-abuzz with the news that Germany, Serbia, and Austria have declared war on Russia. This news worries me. Germany and Turkey have always been close friends, and Russia, their greatest enemy, is just on the other side of the Dersim Mountains—mere days away from here. If Turkey enters the war, we might be in the middle of it.

It is later in the day, and now they are saying that Turkey is gathering up her troops, preparing for war yet again. We've already had two wars in the last couple of years. All men between twenty and forty-five are to report to the army and enlist. If they don't do this within ten days, they will be hunted down and killed. I am so worried about my brother Turabi. Somehow he managed to survive the Balkan Wars, but what are his chances of surviving this new war?

Keghani has two older brothers and she too is sick with fear.

When we reached home after work, Yester's husband Onnig was gone. I thought he was older than forty-five but Yester says he is only forty. Who will be left if all the men go into the army? How many women will become widowed?

Ali, as each day passes, I have learned to respect your mother more. Somehow she could foresee what was best for you. I am so grateful that you are in Canada, where it is safe and where the war will not find you. Stay safe and think of me here, among the widows.

August 10, 1914

Lenore says that it is too dangerous for Keghani and me to go to the hospital on our own. There are too many soldiers in the streets. Civilian men have been captured and imprisoned in makeshift jails for trying to avoid the draft. The worst prison is in a big old building known as the Red Konak. Reverend Emmonds went into the city and visited the men in these prisons, preaching to them to accept Jesus as their savior. The prisoners shouted at him to give them bread instead. He came back, his knees muddied and a sad look on his face. But what was he thinking? Can't he see that these men are starving and desperate? Oh, Ali, why do the missionaries think that the solution to every problem is Jesus?

For one whole day, I paced in my bedroom, wondering and worrying about what was happening beyond the house. I opened up the window and leaned out. I couldn't see much, but I could hear the curses and shouts of angry crowds. Lenore says that some of the people who have been captured manage to escape. I wonder where they will go?

Yester packed up some clothing and food, and tried to find Onnig, but she came back with wild eyes and a torn blouse. I asked her if she found out where he was, but she just sobbed.

Finally, after she had calmed down, she told me what had happened. The captured men were supposed to be turned into soldiers, but they'd been given no uniforms, no weapons, and barely anything to eat. The lucky ones received no more than a small loaf a day. Others had nothing. Yester says they looked pitiful, their clothing was ragged, and there was nowhere to sleep. They had no place to wash—the smell was beyond belief. It wouldn't be long before disease would spread.

Yester was passing by one of the courtyards when a man reached out through the grillwork and grabbed her. She struggled to get away, but he held fast. Another prisoner climbed over the fence and leaped upon her like an animal. He reached for the bread in her pocket and ripped her skirt, then punched her and stole her bundle. She would have died on the spot, but a soldier came along and beat the man back, and she limped away.

I warmed a basin of water and cleaned most of her wounds and bound them with gauze. But nothing will heal her wounded heart. She did not find Onnig.

August 21, 1914

Loud banging on the door woke me at dawn this morning. Through the window I could make out a group of officers. I pulled the curtains shut and stood by my door. The pounding continued. I put my ear to the vent in the floor and listened. Reverend Emmonds answered the door and the soldiers stomped into the house. Then the shouting began. The soldiers demanded that Reverend Emmonds give up the house, so the army can use it for their officers. More shouting. The soldiers left.

An hour later, I found the courage to go downstairs. Reverend Emmonds sat at the kitchen table, still in his nightclothes, his head in his hands.

"How did you get them to leave?" I asked.

"I told them to go to the vali," he said. "America is not at war, so they cannot take over our property."

Yester was nowhere to be seen. I could only guess that she was still in bed, recovering from her beating. I silently brewed a pot of tea for Reverend Emmonds and made him a bowl of porridge. We have no fresh fruit or vegetables left and no way of getting more with all the soldiers in the streets, so I put the remainder of the porridge into another bowl, poured a second cup of tea, and carried it to Yester's room. There was no answer when I knocked. The door wasn't locked, so I opened it quietly. She was still asleep; I left the breakfast tray on her night table.

Lenore rose at her usual time in the morning and seemed not to know about the soldiers' dawn visit. The reverend didn't tell her and I could see that he was trying very hard to be lighthearted for her benefit.

I could not shake the sense that something terrible was about to happen.

Keghani and I made a simple lunch of tea and tinned meat on stale bread—cut in fancy squares and circles to make it look tastier. After our meal, Lenore summoned us all to her sitting room on the second floor. It has a large glass window and in the afternoon, it gets direct sunlight. She gave each of us a piece of tinted glass and told us to look at the sun. As I stared through the glass, I gasped in shock. The sun and the moon approached each other, and then the moon enveloped the sun. All that remained was blackness where the sun should be.

"I cannot watch," I told Lenore, setting the tinted glass down on the table and covering my eyes with my hands.

"Zeynep," she said. "This is a once-in-a-lifetime chance to witness a solar eclipse. Keep on watching. I think you'll be interested in what happens next."

Reluctantly, I raised the tinted glass to the sun once more. Ever so gradually, the moon moved off of the sun, but for the longest time all that remained was a narrow sliver of sun. The crescent moon is a holy sight for Alevis, but a crescent sun? It filled me with dread. Even after the crescent disappeared, and the sun and moon parted from each other, I couldn't shake the feeling that something in our world was about to disintegrate.

August 23, 1914

My premonition was accurate. Entire cities are burning around us.

September 9, 1914

The soldiers have settled in our city. The officers force the drafted men to practice their marching up and down the streets of Harput, making it difficult for us to get around. The officers give their orders in Turkish, and most of the enlisted men understand. But the Alevi Kurds from the Dersim Mountains speak Zaza, not Turkish. They stand there looking puzzled, try-ing to figure out what they're supposed to do. This enrages the officers. Today I saw a boy from the mountains not much older than my brother. When he didn't understand, the officer beat him with a stick. He was bloodied and bruised, but he tried to copy what the other drafted men were doing, so he wouldn't be beaten to death. I wonder how far the men from the Dersim Mountains will be pushed before they push back.

Praise be to God that Turabi speaks Turkish and Armenian as well as Zaza. He will not be beaten because he doesn't un-derstand. He may die regardless, but at least not at the hands of his own commanding officer. I pray that he survives this war.

Lenore made us armbands with a red cross stitched on them, so the soldiers would know we worked at the hospital. Now Keghani and I are back to work. I'm glad that we're back to our routine at the hospital. One ward is reserved for wounded soldiers, but the rest of the hospital is filled almost entirely with women and children who are sick with starvation. Without their menfolk they have no money for food. And the soldiers have long since stolen what the women had been able to hoard. We do what we can for them.

The soldiers go to the market and take whatever they want from the vendors without paying. Some of the shopkeepers have tried locking their doors, but the soldiers just break them down. It is complete chaos here. We are able to get some supplies, so we're not going hungry. I don't know how the Emmonds manage it, but they do. Thank goodness for that.

September 10, 1914

A woman from the Dersim Mountains came into the hospital today, her abdomen bound tightly with a scarf. As soon as she walked through the door, she collapsed in the hallway. I called for help and Dr. Tapalian, one of the Armenian doctors, came running. We lifted her onto an operating table. The scarf was so stiff with blood and dirt that it was nearly cemented to her body.

"Stay and assist me, Zeynep," Dr. Tapalian said as he delicately cut away the top layer of cloth. "You can speak her language."

I stood by and handed him forceps, scissors, and syringes of water. When the final layer of cloth came off, a gaping bayonet wound in her abdomen was revealed, filled with squirming maggots. The sight made me want to vomit.

"She's lucky," said Dr. Tapalian. "If it weren't for those maggots eating away the rotten flesh, she'd be dead."

It took all of my fortitude to breathe slowly and assist Dr. Tapalian as he methodically removed the maggots, disinfected her wound, and sewed her up. When he was finished, I wheeled her into my ward.

She didn't wake until I was almost ready to go home that evening, but I was thankful to still be there for her so she'd have someone to speak to.

"How are you doing?" I asked her in Zaza.

"You are an Alevi like me," she said, her eyes filling with tears. "What is your name?"

"Zeynep. And yours?"

"I'm Esrin." She grabbed my hand and kissed it. "Thank you for saving my life, Zeynep."

"It was Dr. Tapalian who saved your life," I said. "And the maggots."

"An old family cure in times of violence." Esrin squinted as she searched my face. "Where are you from?" she asked.

"Eyolmez."

She nodded. "My great-great-aunt was from Eyolmez."

"Where are you from?" I asked.

"Our village is tucked high in the mountains three days from here," she said, pointing toward Erzurum. "There are Alevi villages all around there. We've been waging war against the government."

"How were you injured?"

"Men fleeing the army seek refuge with us, and we hide them when we can. But last week, soldiers came and took away the hiding men. Then they attacked the villagers. Many of us died."

"I am so sorry," I told her. "Does this mean that you'll stop hiding people?"

Esrin shook her head emphatically. "Never. We cannot give in to this government. We will continue to help, even if we all die in the process."

September 13, 1914

Esrin left yesterday. Before she went, she put her hand on my cheek and said that I was the daughter of her heart. Her words filled me with longing for my own mother. Dr. Tapalian said that Esrin was not healthy enough to leave, but she said that if she stayed in the hospital even one night longer, she would die. I accompanied her down the street and watched as she walked out the city gates. Her progress was slow but determined.

The officers and drafted men are leaving Harput today. They will be marching right through Eyolmez to get to Erzurum, where the fighting is. This frightens me more than I can tell you. The army is like a cloud of locusts, destroying everything in its path. What will become of Mama, Aunt Besee, Cousin Fatma, and the children? What about all my other friends and family? Will the deserters find Esrin's village, and will the soldiers attack it again? I hope Esrin can hide.

Yester, Keghani, and I went out together to see if we could catch a glimpse of our loved ones amid the marching hordes. Yester thought she spotted Onnig and ran up to an old man in rags leaning on a cane, but when she reached him and he turned around, she realized her mistake. I stood on the side of the road and looked at every single man who walked past me, but I didn't recognize anyone—not my brother Turabi, nor Fatma's brother Hassan, nor my old neighbor Riza. Krikor and Shant from the Armenian part of our village were nowhere to be seen either. Perhaps the fact that I've seen none of them is a good sign? Maybe they've all been taken somewhere else. It would be terrible if they were sent to plunder their own home village.

Keghani's face was wet with tears as she stood beside me watching the men march out of the city. All around us, women wailed and tore their clothing, flinging themselves to the ground, but other than the tears, Keghani was still. I admire her courage. It takes such strength of character to hide your emotion in the face of the enemy. I tried to act as strong as Keghani.

It is later, and now I understand Keghani's reaction to the men marching out of the city. She has been keeping a secret. The root cellar beneath the Emmonds' house has a stone wall, and behind that wall Onnig has dug out a hidden room. Yester never knew what her husband was up to, but Keghani knew. All this time when I thought Onnig was gardening, he was actually carrying up dirt from the basement and mixing it into the vegetable beds. Onnig is hiding under the house now, and so is Raffi, Keghani's oldest brother. We don't know where her other brother Toven has gone. He may be hiding somewhere else or the army may have captured him.

Yester was furious with Keghani for keeping Onnig's whereabouts a secret for so long, but I understand why she did it. Because Yester believed her husband was taken, her distress was real. She didn't have to act. It's different with Keghani—people around here probably had no idea she even had brothers to worry about.

Keghani is craftier than I ever realized.

October 2, 1914

At dawn this morning Fatma showed up with Aunt Besee and Suleyman. Baby Zeynep was not with them!

My dear niece and namesake Zeynep has died.

I cannot bear the sorrow. Although I hardly knew her, I thought of her so often. And now she is gone.

Poor Fatma is delirious with grief. Her feet were bloodied to the bone. Reverend Emmonds lifted her into the cart and drove her to the hospital, carrying her into the building in his arms. Aunt Besee is rail thin and her eyes are wild, but she refused to go to the hospital. She stayed behind to be with Suleyman. She refuses to let the boy out of her sight.

"If my grandson dies too, I will kill myself," she said.

October 7, 1914

These days have been filled with sadness. Fatma refused to stay in the hospital for long. I do not blame her; it is a terrifying place, with the sounds of people screaming and weeping all day long, and the smell of blood and rot. It's not uncommon to hear the grinding sounds of a handsaw cutting through bone when amputations are necessary, and there are times when the floors run wet with blood. We try to keep it clean, but it's not always possible with so few helpers and so many people in need. I wish the kings and sultans and revolutionaries who declared this war would come to our hospital for just one day. Maybe if they saw how much their people were suffering, they'd stop their fighting.

Once Fatma's feet were treated and wrapped in gauze, Reverend Emmonds carried her out as gently as he brought her in.

I was afraid that Lenore would be furious that my family had arrived on her doorstep, but she welcomed them. I told her that Fatma, Aunt Besse, and Suleyman could take my bed and I would sleep on the floor, but Lenore wouldn't hear of it. She insisted we all move into her own sitting room on the second floor. She had bedding brought in and arranged on the carpet, so we can sleep together in a circle, as a traditional family would. At night we look out the glorious picture window at the stars and the moon. It isn't the American way and I was surprised that Lenore suggested it. I think she saw what a bad state Fatma was in and felt that this old way of sleeping might soothe Fatma's soul.

On that first night together with the remnants of my family, I gazed out the window at the moon and thought of the last night you and I danced the semah. Back then I had so much to be thankful for, but I didn't appreciate it. Is there anything more important than family? I wish we could dance the semah now, spinning in the moonlight until we are dizzy. It would be like a salve for Fatma's grieving heart to perform our holy dance. But we are all women except for Suleyman—and he's too young to participate. How can we properly worship God without our men beside us? It breaks my heart in two.

Yester has been so kind as well. She haggled for some good cloth at the market and has made a new dress and tunic for Aunt Besee and Fatma, as well as two new outfits for Suleyman. Fatma tried to express her gratitude, but Yester brushed it off, saying she had been waiting for the chance to try out her new Singer sewing machine.

It has taken me a while to get the story out of Fatma and Aunt Besee. When the soldiers marched into Eyolmez, they took over the entire village—both the Armenian and Alevi quarters—kicking people out of their own homes. The soldiers took everything. They broke into the storehouses and stole the grain that had been stored for winter. They vandalized the Petrosians' store, filling their sacks with everything they could get their hands on: groceries, baked goods, even the cups and plates. They ignored Mr. Petrosian's plea to just take what they needed. Petrosian wept as one of the officers opened up the stone oven and even took the cakes that were still baking. As they left, one of the soldiers pointed a gun at Petrosian's face. "Be thankful we didn't kill you."

Now there are hundreds of soldiers occupying our homes. They stationed themselves at the well and wouldn't allow the villagers to draw water. Fatma and Aunt Besee fled to the mountains with the children. You know how hard it is to get water in the mountains at this time of year, Ali. The streams were already frozen. But many of the villagers escaped to the mountains, enduring the cold and thirst and facing starvation. But they were too terrified to stay.

The soldiers have taken over all of the villages in our area. It is hard to imagine

Fatma also told me something that makes no sense: none of the soldiers were Armenian. I know the soldiers took Armenians; we saw it.

Were they sent somewhere else?

Fatma was still breastfeeding Zeynep, and for the first few days while they were hiding in the mountains, Zeynep was fine. But Fatma's milk stopped coming. Without water, there was no milk. Zeynep died in Fatma's arms.

They buried her up there, and for that I am grateful. My dear namesake will have the mountains of Eyolmez to embrace her, and the sun and moon will shine down on her. She will never suffer again and she will be one with the earth. But I miss her so much. She would have grown to be a strong woman, but now she is nothing but dust.

Fatma said that Mama is safe. She refuses to leave the mountains; she is still hoping that Turabi survives the war and comes home. She says if would be terrible if he lived only to find that his family had abandoned him. Mama is tough; she can survive on practically nothing. But dear God, protect my mother from harm.

My trip to Harput had been long and difficult. But since then, thousands of soldiers' feet have beaten a path from Harput to Eyolmez. Fatma, Suleyman, and Aunt Besee took this beaten dirt road to get to me. It was still a treacherous journey, and Fatma had to cover Suleyman's eyes more than once as they passed the corpses of many dead soldiers.

I hate myself for the terrible things I said to Fatma while she was carrying Zeynep. I should never have criticized Fatma for getting pregnant. Can I ever forgive myself for those awful words?

I tried to apologize to Fatma, but she refused to listen. "You and I were both foolish girls," she said. "You were angry with Ali for leaving, and I was jealous of your freedom. I think we're both wiser now."

She's right about that.

October 10, 1914

Oh, Ali.

I don't know how I am ever going to make this right. How I wish I could cross the ocean and get to where you are.

Fatma has finally told me why she owed me an apology.

It wasn't Fatma's fault. She didn't find out until after your mother died. Fatma sorted through your mother's things, including her enameled lap desk. She opened it up and found your letters along with Yousef's. But there was another letter from you that was still sealed.

To me.

Fatma didn't open it. She brought it with her all the way here from Eyolmez.

March 1914

Dear Zeynep,

Ten months have gone by and Yousef has received letters from Fatma. I have sent you letter after letter, but still no word from you. I will say it again: I am sorry I left you behind. I shouldn't have done it. I should have figured out a way to take you with me—just as we had always promised each other.

Work at the foundry in Brantford is difficult and exhausting, but I am saving every penny I can. Once Mama's taxes are paid, the rest will go to a ticket so you can join me. I want this more than anything, Zeynep. I think you'll like it here. There are no mountains in Brantford, but there are trees and gardens and a beautiful river. All the buildings are new here, and the streets are clean. Not far from my rooming house is a public park, where people of all religions are allowed to walk. Sometimes they have fairs and parades and picnics. It's a different life, but a good one. Most important: there are jobs.

Dear Zeynep, please answer me. I wear your evil-eye pendant around my neck as a constant reminder of you. The photograph of you standing before our mountain is my most prized possession. I look at it every night. I am halfway around the world, thinking of you always.

Loving you and hoping you still love me,
Ali

I will cherish this letter with my heart and soul, Ali. Even when you thought I had abandoned you, you kept on writing. How could I ever have doubted you?

But what was your mother thinking? I should be angry, but instead I am sad. How awful for your mother that she died, holding hostage her own son's happiness. Did she destroy all your other letters to me, or did she return them? But she did keep this last one. Perhaps she had a change of heart before the end.

Now the war is on and I cannot reach you. I cannot tell you that I love you always and forever. I cannot hold you close. Every time I see the moon, I think of you. But then again, every time I take a breath I think of you. Every time my heart beats, I think of you.

Please don't give up on me, Ali.

October 17, 1914

When I first came to live with the Emmonds I was amazed that so many rooms held so few people. But now we have a hideaway below the house for Onnig and Raffi, then Yester and Keghani sleep on the main floor, while my family occupies the second floor. Reverend Emmonds and Lenore must sometimes feel that the house is no longer their own.

We have settled into a new routine. Keghani and I still go to the hospital every day, but instead of attending classes in the afternoon, we spend the entire day at the hospital. It is so full of sick and injured people that even the hallways and stairwells are used. There is no fighting in Harput, so you might wonder why the hospital is crowded. Villagers from the war zone come here—mostly women and children who are starving and diseased. And then we receive the wounded soldiers. At first it was just one ward, but each day it seems we have more. My heart goes out to these men who have lost limbs and eyes. On top of that, they too are suffering from malnutrition and disease. If they survive, they'll become a burden to their families. If they die, who will earn money for their wives and children? There is no answer. It is all a disaster.

My main job is to keep ward four sanitized. This ward was built for twelve adults, but now it holds twice as many children. I mop the floors with disinfectant and change the sheets each time a new child arrives. But how can I change the sheets when I run out? Often the shelves in the utility closet are bare. I do the best that I can and I try to stay cheerful. These children have seen horrors and the hospital should be a place of refuge. There are very few doctors here, but Dr. Tapalian makes a point of visiting my ward at least once a day. He's not old but his face looks worn from exhaustion. I think he sometimes sleeps here.

Whenever I can, I sing to the children. By the end of the long day, my throat hurts from singing and my back aches from cleaning. But I've made a difference.

Keghani is in another ward, and she performs the same duties that I do. Fatma stays at home to take care of Suleyman, but she helps by making bandages. I don't blame her for not wanting Suleyman out of her sight.

Aunt Besee helps Yester in the kitchen and they stretch the meager ingredients as far as they can; so in addition to feeding us, there is soup and bread available to the beggars who come to our door. Of course there is also Raffi and Onnig to feed, although the Emmonds don't know about that.

Lenore is at the hospital every day as well. She's isn't a doctor but she is often called upon to perform minor surgeries. There are simply not enough hands to run this place. The reverend comes here too, but all he does is talk about Jesus. If he would roll up his sleeves and help me clean, it would be a much more useful service. He is a kindhearted man and I know that he means well, but can't he understand that God prefers good deeds to hollow words?

I am so grateful that you are in Canada, Ali, and that the war cannot touch you there. Much as I wish we were together, I am happier to know that you are safe.

November 9, 1914

Last week I overheard the Emmonds speaking quietly behind the door of their room. It seems that the rumors are true: Turkey is at war with Russia. This means Anatolia too. We've known that it had to be true, judging from the number of wounded soldiers that have been brought to our hospital, but now it will get even worse. The draft has been expanded. All men between the ages of seventeen and sixty-five are to be made soldiers. Will there be no men left in all of Turkey?

Now the tailors and shoemakers have been rounded up in

the pouring rain, and the soldiers are marching them out of the city to join the army. They are going on foot in this terrible weather and they have no extra food or clothing with them. I fear that they will die along the way.

Some of the missionaries have packed up and left. The army has taken over their buildings. Who will be next? What will happen to us?

In the Emmonds' mailbox this morning was a large packet of returned letters. Yester sorted them and handed one to me. It was the letter I wrote to you in July. It breaks my heart that you did not receive it. Oh, Ali, how I wish there were some way I could talk to you. I miss you with all my heart and soul. I pray to God that you are safe and that you haven't forgotten me.

November 18, 1914

I can hardly believe it, Ali. One of the missionaries told Lenore that a nearby Armenian village was attacked by gangs. Many people were killed, including the Armenian priest. The houses were looted. No one has been charged. The government doesn't care.

Some of the patients were talking about it later, and one person said the Armenians deserved it because they are traitors. It doesn't make sense. Armenians have lived in Anatolia for thousands of years, just like the Alevis. Anatolia is part of Turkey. We all share this country.

How I fear for our future.

PART TWO

Chapter One

KAPUSKASING CAMP, ONTARIO

January 1915

I can barely find the words for the devastation that I feel. All my belongings have been burned.

We each had a carpetbag containing extra clothing and bedding. Inside the bags we also kept our lockboxes with letters, photos, and money. When we arrived at the internment camp, the guards who emptied the train compartments thought the bags were garbage.

They burned everything.

I've lost my one photograph of Zeynep.

I've lost my mother's letters and the letters I wrote to Zeynep that were returned unopened. I've also lost the fifty-two dollars that I had been saving to bring Zeynep to Canada. But I have this journal because I carry it with me always. It reminds me of Zeynep and gives me the illusion of being close to her, even though I may never see her again. And I have her evil eye to keep me safe.

I feel like my past has been seared to nothing.

What will my future hold?

My heart aches with the knowledge that I will never again read my mother's words, but I cannot let go of the hope that I will hear from Zeynep someday. Her evil eye feels so warm right now that I fear it will burn a hole into my chest. I'll take it as a good sign—when her anger burns out, she will still love me. I pray that she is safe, wherever she is. I don't know how much more I can lose.

There is a great war going on, and Canada is in it. Canada's enemy is the Ottoman Empire, along with Germany and Austria. People in Canada who hold citizenship to these countries are suspected of being enemies.

I tried to explain that I am an Alevi and no friend of the Turks who control the Ottoman Empire, but they don't understand. To them, I'm from Turkey, and therefore a Turk.

I am imprisoned in a vast cold wilderness in a place called Kapuskasing Internment Camp. My brother Yousef is here as well, along with ninety-eight other Alevis from Brantford, Ontario. We were brought north by train through cities and towns. When the cities and towns thinned out, the train kept on going through a land of snow and trees and rocks. Once, there was a snowdrift on the track that was so high the train ground to a trembling halt. The soldiers made us dig out the tracks so we could continue the journey to our northern prison. When we climbed back inside the boxcar, I warmed my frozen fingertips over the coal stove and thought of happier times.

After we arrived at the camp, the guards who burned our things apologized. But I don't know if they were sincere; it appeared almost like a joke to them. They were incredulous that what looked like trash to them could possibly be so important to us. The commanding officer made light of the incident, telling us he'd make sure we had an extra package of cigarettes each in compensation. I do not smoke, but he said they could be bartered for goods in the camp store. A sincere apology would have been respectful, but this smirking attitude, as if we were making a fuss over nothing, is difficult to stomach. Nothing will replace the memories that have been taken from us.

While in the midst of mourning the loss of our belongings, we were each given an ax, then marched at bayonet point out into the forest. It was a silent walk, the only sound being the measured stomp of footsteps in snow and the creaking of frozen fir boughs.

As we got deeper into the woods, I stopped thinking about my burned belongings. Instead I was overwhelmed with the sense of how insignificant we humans are. The spruce trees are old, with impossibly tall narrow trunks that sway gracefully in the wind as they reach up to touch the sky. The scent of their spicy, sweet resin reminds me of our mountains and trees back home.

This forest is a holy place. I feel it in my bones. I could have stood there all day looking up to the sky, mesmerized by the rhythmic sway of the tallest branches. Even in that cluster of soldiers and prisoners, I felt alone yet at one with the universe.

"You there," said a camp guard, placing a gloved finger on my shoulder.

The spell was broken.

"Wake up, it's time to get to work. Start with that big one."

It took a moment for his words to sink in. Did he really want me to cut down this spruce tree? To do such a thing was forbidden in my culture. All wildlife is sacred to us—the trees, the deer, the rabbits, even the smallest rodents. To kill wildlife is to steal from God. In Anatolia, our houses were built of stone and mud; and we raised farm animals for food and leather, using their dung as heating fuel. We didn't chop down God's trees and we didn't shoot God's deer or rabbits for food.

I dropped to my knees and gathered up branches that had fallen to the ground—it wouldn't be sinful, as the trees had discarded the branches on their own. "There is plenty of wood here," I said, holding up an armful of branches. "Surely, surely we can gather all we need for fuel from the forest floor instead of killing the trees?"

The soldier looked at me and frowned. "This whole forest is coming down," he said. "You will build your own bunkhouse from this lumber. The rest will be sold down south." He pointed his rifle at my belly. "Get to it."

I gripped my ax and walked up to the majestic tree. I took off my glove, reached up into a branch, and grasped a small seed cone. I held the cone to my nose and breathed in the familiar resin scent. Then I put the cone in my pocket, placed my hand on the gray bark of the trunk, and prayed. God is the sun, the moon, the stars—and all of nature. Could I really destroy this magnificent spruce for no reason except to make a prison for myself? But if I didn't, this man would shoot me. Would he then shoot my brother and all my friends? I wrapped both arms around the trunk and rested my cheek on its bark, ignoring the prickling needles as they brushed against my skin.

The guard was wordless for a moment, but then he sighed deeply. Finally, he said, "We're here to clear out the trees, not make love to them."

His words infused me with sadness. To him, this was not a sacred object but just a piece of wood. He would never understand the magnitude of what he expected me to do. I took a deep breath and let it out slowly, then released the trunk and stood back. I picked up my ax and regarded the soldier. Could I blame him for his orders? Not really. His duty was a practical one: to make sure we would cut down enough wood so we could build our bunkhouse.

I turned back to the tree. "Forgive me, God," I whispered under my breath.

With every ounce of strength I had, I swung the ax into the

spruce tree, hacking at the same vulnerable spot on its trunk over and over again, until the whole tree crashed down into the snow.

When I finished, I was covered in a sheen of sweat and guilt. "Good job," said the guard. "But you'll never finish a day's work if you hug every tree before you cut it down."

I lost count of how many trees I cut down that first day in the woods, but I never lost the feeling that I was committing a sin. We worked until dark, then marched back to camp, ice on our eyebrows and beards, our hats and shoulders covered in snow.

The tents were more substantial than I would ever have guessed and each one was big enough to hold the same sixteen men as each boxcar. This meant that Yousef and I would stay together. We were issued blankets and sheets.

Before we arrived at this camp in the wilderness, we were briefly imprisoned at Fort Henry, a stone fortress in a city called Kingston. Most of the prisoners were Ukrainians, but there were some Germans as well. We Alevis were in the minority.

The Germans called the Ukrainians "Austrian scum." They called us "dirty Turks." Nobody understands who we are; it has been a problem ever since we arrived in Canada. After we got off the ship, the Canadian customs official asked my nationality. I told them I was an Alevi Kurd. He looked at me oddly and said, "You're from Turkey, so are you Armenian or Turkish?" I told him I was Kurdish. With exasperation, he asked if I was Christian or Muslim. I told him I was neither. "Are you Jewish then?" he asked, his pen poised over a little box on his form.

"No, I said. "I'm *Alevi*."

He shook his head and wrote "Turk" in that little box. In some ways that's the truth. We Alevi Kurds are the original inhabitants of Turkey. We hid in the mountains when invaders came to kill us. When we pray, it's in Zaza, not Arabic, like the Muslims. But these Canadians think that anyone from the Ottoman Empire who isn't Christian must be Muslim. They don't seem to know about the Alevis, who were in Anatolia long before Turkey existed.

The Ukrainians had the same problem. The Canadians thought they were Austrian.

The Germans at Fort Henry were military men and, in truth, were the only true enemies of Canada; yet for some reason they were given special treatment. They didn't have to work, they received better food, they were even allowed to put on plays and sports competitions. But they protested the fact that they had to share a prison with the "lower classes" like us and the Ukrainians. Why did the camp guards listen to them? First they shipped out a group of Ukrainians to Kapuskasing, and then they shipped out the Alevis.

As we came back from that first day of killing trees and began to put up our tents, I recognized Bohdan, a Ukrainian prisoner from Kingston who had always been quite friendly. He hurried over to help us with the tents.

"There was nothing up here except for the station house when we arrived," he said. "We lived in the train cars for the first few days."

"How do you like it up here?" I asked.

He shrugged. "Better than Fort Henry. At least we're away from those Germans. But the work is hard here, and it's so cold." He pulled out a thick wad of newspaper from inside his coat and handed it to me. "Stuff your boots with this," he said. "Otherwise you'll get frostbite."

There was enough for Yousef as well. "Thank you," I said.

"I'd invite you to come to our bunk for supper," said Bohdan. "But I don't think you'd like what we're having—pork stew."

"Thank you for the offer," I said, trying hard to keep the disgust off my face. I had never seen a pig until I came to Canada, and they seemed like such dirty animals. "We'll stick with our rice and cheese and vegetables."

"Suit yourself," he said, not unkindly.

Later, I could feel my hands, face, and feet gradually thaw as we huddled around the tent's wood stove and ate our plain supper. After the meal, Bohdan came back with some of his friends. They carried fir boughs and long pliable branches. "You can each make yourself a comfortable bed with these," he said.

They showed us how to fashion a frame with the branches and a surprisingly comfortable mattress and pillow by using the fir boughs as stuffing. After they left, I stretched out on my new bed and closed my eyes. I was comfortable and warm and surrounded by the scent of spruce resin. But the scent no longer reminded me of home—now it reminded me that I was a prisoner, forced to do things that were against my beliefs. I felt only sadness and shame.

I closed my eyes and listened to the drifts of conversation of my tent-mates, but after a while their voices faded and I thought of how I got into this situation in the first place.

Chapter Two

BRANTFORD, ONTARIO, 1914

When the war started last year, all foreigners working in Brantford were let go for "patriotic reasons." Soon foreigners were begging in the downtown area. The police in turn began to look out for anyone they described as disturbing the peace.

I never begged, but with nothing to do, I wandered the streets near our boarding house. One day I walked by the newly built post office, which seemed too big for such a little city, with its six-storied clock tower and broad granite steps. Jack Olinsky, also newly fired from the foundry, sprawled on the bottom step, oblivious to the disapproving looks of the well-dressed people who stepped past him to get inside. A police officer named Casey grabbed his elbow and took him away.

I slipped into the alleyway behind the post office so the officer wouldn't see me once he had finished dealing with Jack. And that's how I discovered a neglected courtyard almost completely enclosed by the backs of the windowless buildings. Silence surrounded me, and the sky stretched out above my head. I took a deep breath.

Since arriving in Canada, I hadn't been able to perform the ritual semah. But this quiet courtyard, with the sky overhead and the walls shielding me from prying eyes, was the perfect place. There were no Alevi women in Brantford, however. There were probably no Alevi women in all of Canada. How could I perform our dance-prayer?

I closed my eyes and thought back to my last semah. Mama had taken part, and so had Zeynep—six men and six women dancing the intricate steps as if we were spokes of a wheel. We had danced in a circle, turning, twirling, and always the same distance apart. With that vision in my head, I hummed the prayer and swayed to the rhythm plucked out on the bağlama. It was like stepping back in time. Of its own volition, my body took up the precise movements of the ritual dance, swirling and circling in perfect unity with the ghosts of my past. This dance had been performed by generations over thousands of years, before the time of Allah and before the time of Christ. I was like a planet swirling around the sun, a human at one with God. I was alone, but I danced with all the people who had come before me, and my worries began to slip away.

"What are you doing?"

The spell was broken. The other dancers vanished. I opened my eyes.

"Officer Casey," I said. "I wasn't doing anything wrong."

"You weren't putting a curse on our new post office, were you, fella?"

"Nothing of the sort," I said, feeling dizzy and disoriented. My mind hadn't quite made the full transition back to the present. "I was enjoying the space back here. It's so quiet—unusual for the middle of downtown."

"Are you an illegal?" he asked.

"No," I replied, fumbling for my wallet in my back pocket. "I'm not a citizen yet, but my papers are in order." I drew out my Enemy Alien card and handed it to him.

Officer Casey glanced at the card and handed it back. "That's good," he said with a condescending smile. "And you're not in trouble. It's not against the law to appreciate silence, or to dance in circles, but it's better if you do it on your own property. You don't want to give people the wrong idea."

With that, he ushered me down the alleyway and back onto the sidewalk. "Keep moving is my advice to you, fella," he said. "That way, no one will complain."

His use of "fella" grated on my nerves. Since arriving, I found that if I could get Canadians to call me by my name, they saw me more as an individual rather than one of many foreigners.

"Thank you, Officer Casey," I said, inclining my head slightly as a show of respect. "My name is Ali Hassan."

"Ali? That's an unusual name. You might want to call yourself Alex to blend in more. Now be on your way."

Officer Casey wouldn't have realized how offensive his suggestion was. My name was in honor of Ali, Muhammad's son-in-law, Heir and Prophet.

I spent the rest of the day walking, walking, walking. I was afraid to stop, afraid to be accused of loitering. I found a copper and a nickel, and a basket of rotting apples in the waste bin behind the greengrocers'. I didn't really know what to do with them, but figured anything could be boiled and eaten.

That night I went to bed wondering what the next day would bring, hoping that the war would end soon. But I had barely drifted off to sleep when heavy footsteps pounded through the hallway, waking me up.

The door burst open, and the blinding beam of a flashlight penetrated the darkness.

I bolted out of bed, shielding my eyes from the painfully bright light. "Who's there?"

"Police," a familiar voice shouted. Officer Casey. "Get up now. You're all under arrest."

"For what?

"For attempting to blow up the post office."

I fumbled about, pulling on my trousers and shirt. I couldn't find my socks, so I shoved my bare feet into my work boots and grabbed my coat. Officer Casey ushered me out the door. Yousef was a few footsteps behind me.

As we stood in the hallway, I could see the other policemen

flush the boarders from the rest of the rooms.

Soon, all twelve of us were shivering in the street. A soft-bellied policeman tapped his club rhythmically against the palm of one hand as he kept an eye on us. Casey was still inside with the other officers.

Our landlord Hagop Gregorian lived with his wife Arsho and their four children in a small house beside ours. As we stood shivering in the street, Hagop opened his front door and took in the scene. Then he marched over to the policeman who was guarding us.

"Officer Jackson," he said. "What's all this ruckus about?"

"Bomb threat," said the policeman. He pointed his billy club in our direction. "We got a tip that these men were planning the attack."

"I can vouch for them all. They are peaceful and hardworking. They would never do anything like what you're suggesting."

"Sorry to disagree with you. Our information came from Ottawa."

Hagop frowned. "About *these* men?"

"Not just them. All the Turks," said Officer Jackson. "They're the enemy."

"These men are from Turkey, but they're no more Turkish than I am," said Hagop. "They fled for a better life in Canada."

"Not Turkish?" Officer Jackson's wrinkled. "You mean these are Armenians?"

"They're Alevi Kurds," said Hagop. "Friends and neighbors to Armenians. And persecuted by the Turkish government almost as often as the Armenians. Do you think I would rent rooms to people I don't trust?"

Officer Jackson smirked. "Maybe we should arrest all the Armenians too."

Hagop's mouth opened, but no sound came out. He took a deep breath, and drew himself up tall. "I think Ottawa will vouch for the loyalty of Armenians in Canada. Surely you don't think any of us would be on the side of the Turkish government?"

"I know nothing about it," said the policeman. "I just do as I'm told. Now let me get on with it."

Just then, Officer Casey came out of the rooming house. "The other men will continue with the search, Jackson," he said. "You and I will take these men to the jail."

Casey nudged us forward in a group. "Single file."

The last thing I saw before turning the corner was Hagop rushing into our rooming house. I thought of my strong box of precious letters and cash. I prayed that Hagop's presence would keep the police respectful of our meager possessions.

At the jailhouse, we were taken in and processed one at a time while the rest of us shivered outside. When it was my turn, I stepped into a small receiving area that smelled of old food and misery. A bored-looking man in a wrinkled suit filled out a form with my name and age and address. "Are you a Canadian citizen?" he asked.

"Not yet," I answered.

"Too bad," he said, stamping my paper with a loud *thunk*. "You'll be in cell nine."

I followed him down the hallway and stepped inside the small cell. He slid the bars shut and clicked the lock in place. My knees buckled, and I sat on a cold metal bench.

I stared out through the bars as my brother Yousef was locked into the cell beside me. As cells scraped open and clanged shut, a wave of panic surged through me. When I was laid off I thought that my life couldn't get much worse. How wrong I had been.

The next morning, the guard dipped a tin cup into the bucket and drew out some water. "Drink up," he said. "You're not the only one who is thirsty."

It is not the Alevi way to gulp down water without thinking, so I took small sips, ignoring the guard's glare. The water felt soothing on my dry throat. I handed the cup back through the bars.

When they finally let us outside, the sunlight was blinding. I rubbed my eyes and squinted at the sight in front of me. I wondered if it was a mirage. Soldiers in light brown uniforms with brass buttons, two dozen or more of them, fanned out around us, their bayonets poised. Were we that dangerous?

We clustered together in confused groups of twos and threes, talking quietly. More soldiers escorted a second group of men from inside the jail. With them was Boulos Sarout, a full head taller than anyone else. Boulos was from Lebanon and he had been in Brantford since 1900. Like Hagop, he'd saved enough to buy a house and bring his wife and daughters here. He owned Angel Confectionery on Dalhousie Street and his handmade sweets were very popular. Even the mayor shopped at Angel's. Boulos had an aura of quiet authority. It surprised me that he had been arrested.

The soldiers herded us into single file and marched beside us with their bayonets balanced on their shoulders. One of the officers—a colonel—led the way, and a lieutenant walked behind us all. Boulos was first in line, just in front of me. Yousef came next. I felt like a part of a very long snake. They marched us south down Market Street, past Victoria Park. My face burned with shame and I kept my gaze down, but I couldn't help noticing the women who stopped and stared at us, whispering. Gradually, both sides of the street filled with all sorts of people who watched us with curiosity and not much sympathy—laborers with lunch buckets on the way to work, lawyers and businessmen wearing warm coats for the November chill, the clerk from the paint store on Dalhousie Street.

My face reddened as the soldiers escorted us down past the main shopping area in town. It shamed me to be judged by these onlookers. Not only had I been arrested, but I was dirty and disheveled as well. We'd barely been given time to throw on clothing in the middle of the night, and then we'd slept in smelly cramped cells. What did these onlookers think of us? That we were dirty ungrateful foreigners, here to steal jobs from them? They probably had no trouble believing we'd tried to blow up the post office.

As we walked past Angel's Confectionery, the glass door opened and Mrs. Sarout stepped out. Her eyes were red from weeping, but she held her head high and nodded to her husband as he walked past. Boulos's younger daughter flew out the door.

"Get back in here, Marie," said Mrs. Sarout.

Marie ignored her mother. She ran up to her father and tugged on his elbow.

"Papa, I'm so worried about you."

"Go back inside with your mother," said Boulos.

The colonel turned and smiled at Marie, but he didn't slow his pace. "It's fine, Boulos. Your daughter can walk with you."

"Thank you for that kindness, Sergeant Bolt," said Boulos.

It shouldn't have surprised me that they knew each other. Who *didn't* buy candy at Angel's?

Boulos reached out and squeezed his daughter's hand. "I cannot fault you for your bravery, my dear girl."

Marie was silent as she took large steps to keep in pace with her father. I marveled at her poise and determination. She had been born in Beirut and raised strictly, but ever since she, her younger sister, and mother had come to Brantford, they had slowly shed their traditional ways. It must have been a very difficult adjustment for them, but now, a stranger would assume they'd been born in Brantford.

Boulos looked down at his daughter, "Your presence comforts me, Marie. When we get to our destination, have your mother bring my citizenship papers, and tell her to contact our lawyer."

Marie nodded.

When we reached the corner of Dalhousie Street and Brant Avenue, it was clear where we were heading: the Brantford Armoury, which loomed in front of us like a fortress.

We were kept there overnight, but they fed us bread and

jam with strong coffee and gave us blankets. And they brought us our possessions from the boarding house. I didn't blame the soldiers. It was wartime and they had their orders. Then, for the third time in as many days, we marched through the streets of Brantford yet again.

Boulos had been released so now I was the first in line. Unlike the previous two times, I was no longer embarrassed by the situation. I had done nothing to deserve this arrest and I could do nothing to stop it, so I held my head high and nodded politely to the people in the crowd. Some of them waved. A young girl threw a flower that landed at my feet. "Good luck," she called out. I turned to her and smiled.

It wasn't just the crowd's reaction that was different this time. Now, instead of being herded to prison, we were being ushered out of town. All my worldly goods were packed tightly in the blanket that I carried on my back. The soldiers who held their bayonets at the ready were the same ones who had brought us bread and strawberry jam. I wasn't afraid of them and I didn't resent them. Tom Smith, the soldier who marched a few steps ahead of me, had worked in the foundry beside me. He'd only been there for a few weeks when war was declared. His older brother Hank, who had also worked in the foundry, was already overseas. They were prisoners of this war as much as I was.

As we walked down West Street, the train station came into view. Already, the train was waiting for its ninety-eight prisoners. As I put my foot onto the bottom step, Tom stood behind me and steadied my bundle, giving me a boost. I pulled myself up the rest of the steps, then walked down the aisle, taking a seat by the window. Yousef entered next, and he sat down beside me, our bundles resting on the seats in front of us. The rest of the men settled in. Then around thirty soldiers got on the train as well, and they stationed themselves throughout the train cars, their bayonets poised. As the train pulled away, I looked out the window at the growing crowd, wondering if I'd ever come back here again.

PART THREE

Harput, Anatolia

January 14, 1915

A new year has arrived, Ali, and still there is no end to war in sight. I have been too busy and disheartened to write a word. Each day has been more of the same, but today, they sent me home early because I have influenza. Lenore put me back in my old bedroom, so I wouldn't infect Aunt Besee and Fatma, and especially not Suleyman.

I am bundled in blankets, but I cannot seem to get warm.

March 30, 1915

I cannot believe all the time that I've lost. It wasn't just influenza, but typhus. I ached all over, and then I broke out into spots. Fatma and Suleyman stayed away for their own safety, but Aunt Besee was by my side night and day. She bathed me with cold cloths and rubbed my sore joints. She fed me spoonfuls of broth and hugged me when I wept.

Ali, they've cut off all my beautiful long hair. They said it could spread the disease. It will grow back eventually, but when I look in the mirror, the person who stares back at me has dark circles under her eyes and hair that sticks up like a scarecrow. Will you still love me if I'm ugly? The typhus left me weeks ago, yet still every muscle and joint in my body aches. How I long to hold little Suleyman in my arms, but I do not dare. Aunt Besee says that Suleyman misses me. He has drawn pictures of our mountains and Aunt Besee has hung them on the wall. Even though I cannot see Suleyman, it comforts me to look upon these pictures and to know that he is healthy and happy.

I have asked about the war, but they will not tell me. I think they're afraid I'll be upset by the news and it will affect my health. What they don't seem to realize is that not knowing is even worse. What news of the war do you get in Canada, Ali? Maybe you haven't heard about it at all.

April 9, 1915

They let me out of my room and Suleyman was allowed to sit on my lap. I sat in the kitchen with all my family around me and we ate a simple meal together. My heart nearly burst with joy. Suleyman may be your brother's son, but he has your eyes, Ali. When he looks at me, all I can think of is you.

I am so utterly tired. I had to go back to bed for the afternoon. It frustrates me to be so weak. It bothers me that my family is keeping me in the dark about the war. Fatma says I am to concentrate on getting better.

Since my own family will not tell me what's happening with the war, I asked Keghani. She said that soldiers in terrible condition have trickled back from the front to the hospital. They talk among themselves when Keghani is nearby. Maybe they don't realize she can understand Turkish. They talked about the Armenian soldiers, and now I realize why none of them were seen in Erzurum. The Armenians were never sent to fight. Instead, they were killed by the Turkish army.

This is stunning news. Why would an army kill its own soldiers? It makes no sense.

I am so thankful that Raffi and Onnig are safe in their hiding place. I worry about Keghani's other brother. These are terrifying times.

April 10, 1915

I have been thinking about what Keghani has said and it frightens me to the core. When the Sultan ruled, he would blame the Armenians or us any time there was a problem. I was very excited when the Young Turk government came into power because they promised equality for everyone, but more and more all I hear is people saying, "Turkey is for the Turks." We Alevi Kurds and the Armenians have been here since before there *was* a Turkey. Aren't we more Turkish than the Turks?

It takes all my effort to drag myself out of bed and get washed and dressed, but I am determined to return to the hospital and help in any way that I can. But when I tried to accompany Keghani today, she stopped me. "Do you want to get sick again?" she asked. "Typhus is raging at the hospital."

"Then I'm the one who should go," I said. "I won't catch it twice."

She refused to listen, but called Fatma, who held me back while Keghani left. So I am stuck in the house making bandages with Fatma instead of helping where I am most needed. At least I can spend time with dear little Suleyman. Fatma has given him small jobs like stacking and boxing the bandage rolls. He is very good at counting for a five-year-old.

When Fatma put Suleyman down for a nap, Lenore sat down with me. Her eyes were lined with dark circles and her forehead seemed permanently creased. I asked her what she knew about the war. We have a telephone in this house and missionaries from different parts of Turkey call Lenore. From what she's heard, it's true that the Armenians are targeted by the government.

"But why?"

"They want everyone in Turkey to have one religion and nationality," she said. "Armenian officers in the Turkish army have been rounded up and shot. They've let convicts out of the prisons and put them into army uniforms—and these criminal gangs are encouraged to plunder Armenian homes."

Lenore picked up a roll of gauze and stared at it. "While you were sick, a government delegation from Constantinople traveled across the area to speak in mosques. They told the Turks who live among us that Armenians are the enemy and they must be destroyed."

"What about Keghani and Yester?" I asked. "Are they safe?"

"We will do everything that we can to protect them," she said. "The fact that they're women helps. And Keghani is need-ed in the hospital."

"Are the missionaries safe?" I asked her. "You're Christian too."

"They don't dare touch us."

"Why not?"

"The Americans aren't in the war and the Ottoman gov-ernment knows better than to threaten American citizens in Turkey. If they did, it might bring the Americans into the war."

Lenore set down the roll of gauze and left the kitchen. As I sat there, digesting what she had told me, I thought about Onnig and Raffi, hiding in the root cellar. How safe were *they*?

When Fatma came back from the bedroom, I told her about what Lenore had said.

"You missed so much," she said. "While you were sick, soldiers came here and ordered Keghani and Yester to stand in the street while they went through their rooms, searching for guns, but of course they found nothing. I was petrified that they'd discover the secret room in the root cellar. The soldiers said they'd shoot the Armenians in our house who didn't hand over their guns within twenty-four hours."

"But they didn't *have* any guns," I said.

Fatma nodded. "There was no way around it. When Reverend Emmonds came home and heard about this, he went out. He came back an hour later with two rifles—useless things that were falling apart—that he'd bought from a Turk. He gave one to Keghani and the other to Yester, so they'd have something to hand in."

I'm sure many Armenians ended up doing the same thing, but then wouldn't these weapons be used as proof that they were planning an insurrection?

April 15, 1915

Keghani found her brother Toven, which is the best news we've had in a long time. Unfortunately, he is in the Red Konak prison.

Reverend Emmonds went to the prison with her this afternoon to seek Toven's release, but it was no use. The Army says he is a traitor. Keghani says that he is just a shy mathematics student who wants to be a teacher. She can't imagine him ever being a traitor. When Keghani and the reverend returned, she was hysterical with fear so Reverend Emmonds told us what was happening. The Red Konak is filled with men of all backgrounds, but what they have in common is that the government thinks they are traitors. To be thrown into the prison is nearly a death sentence in itself. They don't feed you and the cells are filthy and crowded. Dear God, please keep Toven safe from typhus. Please keep him safe from the army. Please keep him safe from war.

April 16, 1915

Keghani and the reverend were not allowed into the prison today. Instead, they were ushered into the officers' building and told to wait. From there, they had a full view of the prison yard filled with men chained together by iron rings around their necks. Many of them were so sick and thin that they could barely stand, and so they were being dragged by the men who were chained beside them. Keghani and the reverend watched as the door was opened and the prisoners were herded out onto the street. Keghani screamed when she saw Toven limp past, his neck pulped and chafed bloody by the iron ring. His eyes met hers and he called out, "May Jesus be with you, sister." An officer beat him with a stick for that.

Keghani nearly collapsed, but Reverend Emmonds held her up, and asked an officer, "What's happening to those men?"

"They're being sent to Erzurum to fight," said the officer.

"But some of them can barely stand."

"They're healthy enough. They're just putting on a show to get out of doing their military service."

But of course the officer was lying. Keghani has already heard what happens to Armenians who are sent to Erzurum. Her brother will be shot.

April 18, 1915

Yester has taken ill with what looks like influenza. I hope that she doesn't have typhus. Aunt Besee, who does the cooking now, asked me to take food down to Onnig and Raffi in their hiding place. I hadn't been down there for quite a while and was anxious to see how they were doing. The room behind the stone wall has a mud floor, walls, and ceiling, so it is damp and cold. They each have their own bench to sleep on and there's an upturned wooden box in the middle of the room that they use as a table. They mostly play cards or sleep. It must be boring, but at least they are safe.

In addition to the entrance that I already knew about, Onnig showed me another secret project they had been working on: a cleverly disguised tunnel hidden in the ceiling.

"Where does it go to?" I asked.

"The outhouse," he said. "If worse comes to worst, we can escape up through that."

The thought of tunneling up through the outhouse is disgusting, and it makes me think twice every time I use it, but it's preferable to death, and I thought they were smart to create an escape route.

Onnig has lost weight, but he seemed to be healthy. Raffi was upset about Toven's capture, and even though he and Onnig are thankful to be safe, they're worried about their families and neighbors.

Dear God, keep Onnig and Raffi safe.

April 20, 1915

I am still extremely weak from the typhus, but I cannot sit at home anymore. Keghani and I went to the hospital, but when I stepped inside I barely recognized it. Half of the wards are used for typhus patients, and Keghani told me that a third of them die within a few days. Yesterday, one of the female doctors died of typhus, and two nurses who have come down with it are still recovering. I was lucky to recuperate at home and under Aunt Besee's loving ministrations.

The hospital doesn't have enough room for all the sick and wounded, so the army converted the missionaries' Protestant church into a hospital. The patients there have no bedding and no food. It's like they've been dumped off to die. Officers who guard the doors turn away visitors bringing food because it would make the government look bad.

May 1, 1915

Soldiers went door-to-door today, searching Christian houses for weapons and any bit of paper that proves a person is a traitor. I was terrified that they would find this journal. I haven't said anything against the government, but even talking about starving soldiers might be considered treason. I'm glad I hid it in the root cellar with Raffi and Onnig because the soldiers confiscated Yester's recipe book and Reverend Emmonds' sermons. Thankfully they did not find our secret room in the root cellar, so Onnig and Raffi are still safe. The reverend and Lenore still don't know about it, which is for their own good. The reverend has a habit of blurting out things that may be true but are definitely not timely.

The soldiers found an Armenian hiding in the house across the road and I watched from my window as he was taken away. The soldiers bolted the door, then set the house on fire. I hope and pray that the people inside have a secret way out. Lenore says this is happening in all the towns around us.

May 5, 1915

The officers came here again today and took most of our blankets and bedding. They opened up the kitchen cupboards and took all sorts of food. They say it's for the soldiers, but I know that's a lie. I've seen the prison. The soldiers are starving.

May 13, 1915

Typhus is still raging. People are no longer carried on stretchers to the hospital or to the graveyard. Now a cart, piled up with bodies, goes up and down the streets. The gravediggers cannot keep up with the deaths, so the army has taken a house close to the cemetery for storing bodies until they can be buried. This is gruesome beyond words. We try to keep as clean as we can here, and so far no one else in our house has taken ill. Dear God, protect us all.

The epidemic has not stopped the soldiers from raiding houses, looking for guns and Armenians. They've even thrown some Armenian women and girls into the prison, but so far those who live with the missionaries have been safe. Will these women and girls be sent to Erzurum in neck chains to be shot like their men?

Hatred toward the Armenians increases each day. Even in the hospital patients whisper their hatred of Armenians and Christians. I find this strange, since it is Christians who are the doctors and nurses here. One starved soldier who nearly lost an eye muttered to me, "This is a war between Christian nations, yet we're the ones being killed. The Armenians are going to rise up against us."

Keghani said that this is typical, that the Armenians are always blamed. She says it's like the issue of the guns: if they don't find them, the Armenians are accused of hiding them; if they do find them, the Armenians are accused of hiding them. Either way, they will be blamed. The Europeans start a war and the Armenians die because of it.

Ever since this war began, I've had a growing sense of dread. We are holding on day by day, but it's hard to even think that there can be a future. I admire Mama hiding out in the mountains on her own, determined to be there for Turabi if he survives. Ali, are you determined like my mother? Please don't give up on me.

PART FOUR

KAPUSKASING, ONTARIO, FEBRUARY 1915

It's been a year and a half since I came to Canada and in all that time I have not heard a word from you, Zeynep. You cannot write to me now because of the war, but I wonder if that even makes a difference? If you had written to say that you despise me, it would have been preferable to this silence. Sometimes I think you are only a dream, but I cannot sleep for worrying about you and our homeland. Why did you leave our village? Would you have been safer staying in Eyolmez or are you safer now? I wish I knew more about what made you leave. Were you in danger? We thought that when the Young Turks took power it would be a good thing for people like us; that they would fight for equality and take religion out of politics. If only they had done what they said. News trickles through that the

Turks are still in charge and anyone from smaller cultures and religions, like us, the Armenians, and the Greeks, still have no say. The only thing that's changed is that every nationality gets drafted into the army, which makes me worry about our friends and family.

The guards talk about the heavy battles between the Russians and Turks in the Armenian campaign. You can't have gone too far from the mountains dividing Turkey and Russia. I fear that you are in the midst of this war. How will you stay safe? It's driving me mad. If only I were there to protect you.

Since I can't find out about you, I'll tell you about me. We built our prison camp in the northern wilderness on the bank of a mighty river called the Kapuskasing. Bohdan says that the name is a Cree word for "bend in the river"—and we are on the very spot where the river bends, so maybe that's true. The Cree are the original people who lived here. The camp store sits beside railway tracks that run right past our camp. The soldiers measured and staked the outline for a double enclosure of barbed wire, but because the ground is frozen, they can't put the posts in yet. We sleep and eat inside what will be the enclosed part. The parade grounds will be behind barbed wire as well. Each week, more prisoners are brought up here by train, which means more wood is needed to build more bunkhouses.

Those of us from Turkey have been separated from the other prisoners, and I am relieved. Some of the others smell of roasted pig, which is revolting. Each bunkhouse holds 200 men, but there are only 117 of us, so we have plenty of room.

One hundred of us are from Brantford, and the rest are from other cities. We do our own cooking and washing. Some of the prisoners are friendly, but some are angry brutes; they pick fights with us just because we speak a different language and pray differently from them.

We're awoken at 5:30 a.m. in the dark. I have just enough time to eat some cold leftover rice and get dressed. It went down to minus 26 degrees Fahrenheit a few days ago. I wear tight wool trousers called long johns underneath my overalls and an undershirt and shirt, with a hat, coat, and gloves over top it all. The wind and cold get through this clothing very quickly, and I am frozen all day long. We have been issued boots and socks, and I line my boots with paper for warmth. It doesn't help much.

At six, the prisoners assemble in the parade grounds in the center of the internment camp. We stand shivering in rows while the soldiers check our names off their list to make sure that no one has escaped during the night.

Some people have tried, but where would they go? We're in the middle of the wilderness. An escapee would either freeze to death or be killed by a bear or wolf. There are thirty guards with dogs patrolling day and night. I wonder why they bother putting up the barbed-wire fencing.

One man caught trying to escape was punished with one week's isolation on Prison Island, which is in the middle of the river just beyond the camp. He was marched down to the pier, where two guards took him across the water by boat. The prison is a small wood cabin. I saw him after. His cheeks were gaunt and his eyes were crazed. I never want to go there.

After roll call, we are organized into work teams. Since I've been here, my work team has been assigned to the exact same job every day: cutting down magnificent trees by hand with an ax. The soldiers call this "cutting posts"—even the term shows their disrespect for nature. Don't they know that trees are more than just dead posts?

When we first got here, my team would cut down trees close to the camp in order to make the camp bigger. They were loaded onto a flatbed wagon and taken to other work teams to make into planks, which would then be used to build bunk-houses and other buildings. More prisoners are brought to the camp every week, so we have to cut down more trees for more bunkhouses. It's exhausting work and we do this all day with just a short lunch break at noon to eat whatever we brought with us. By the time we march back to camp, it's dark again. The daylight does not last long here in the winter.

We have cut down so many trees that there is a clearing all around our camp, making it look like one huge, ugly wound on the earth. At least our bunkhouses are warmer than the tents, although little stops the wind howling through the cracks. I've tried filling the cracks with spruce resin, which helps, but it is an incredibly tedious job. It's so cold that the resin freezes before I can get it into the crack. This cold bites through to the bone.

Now that we've cleared this vast area all around the camp, our group is marched deeper into the woods each day. It is backbreaking and soul breaking. Such ugliness and destruction, Zeynep. Officer Wilkin, who oversees us, doesn't seem to be bothered by it. All around there are just stumps and bare earth covered with our snowy, muddy footsteps, yet Wilkin smiles. And as for the cold, he says we should be grateful for it. "The black bears stay asleep as long as you're freezing," he said. "Count yourselves fortunate." What kind of man is he?

I am ashamed to admit that I've become very good at cutting down trees. The air is filled with the scent of resin, but when I smell it, my stomach churns as though it's the scent of blood on battlefields. How close are you to the battlefields, Zeynep?

Your ghost visited me, Zeynep. My ax was poised to attack a majestic jack pine whose limbs resembled a woman's outstretched arms. Just before my blade hit the trunk, I saw a flash of red. I stopped the ax, and then dropped it in the snow.

A single thread of red cloth had caught in the bark, reminding me of the silk that you wear in your hair. I removed my glove and pulled the thread from the tree. I held it up to my face, hoping to breathe in your scent, but it was so insubstantial that it was like trying to get a whiff of a ghost. I wound it around my baby finger and put my glove back on. I didn't cut that tree down. It would be like taking an ax to you.

By the end of the day, all the trees around it had been felled. It stood alone like a banished widow in the snow.

When the lights are out in our bunkhouse, I lie here on my mattress stuffed with pine boughs and think of you. When I hold this red thread up to my cheek my heart is filled with sadness. What does it mean that it smells of nothing? Where are you, Zeynep? Are you safe? Do you ever dream of me?

Wilkin and his men only stayed an hour in the woods with us this morning, Zeynep.

Their coats are sturdier than ours and they wear sweaters hand-knit by their wives underneath, yet they still shiver. I know a way that they could warm up: they could work as hard as we do. Instead, they trek back to the camp where they probably sit around a warm stove, drink coffee, and complain about how lazy we are. In truth, we give them as little work as we possibly can. We're prisoners after all, and our labor is only to make room for more prisoners.

My head ached from the sound of so many trees being hacked down, so I walked into a denser part of the woods where there was no damage yet. As I stood there in the cold silence, I looked at the sky and savored the majesty of this universe. I looked down at the fresh snow and noticed how it sparkled like jewels in the sun. The trees themselves stood silently around me, their branches stretched out, as if in supplication, robed in glittering white. If I had come to this place as a free man instead of a prisoner, I could grow to love it. After the war, Zeynep, would you cross the ocean to be with me? Maybe we could find a wilderness like this that isn't yet destroyed by greedy men. Maybe we could live off the land, just the two of us.

A movement caught my eye and fear surged through me.

Only days ago, a prisoner saw huge, clawed footprints in the snow, so I was on edge. I turned. Nothing.

I stood perfectly still, breathing so slowly that no puffs of air would show in the cold, hoping to blend in with the trees so the creature would move on. Suddenly, I spied a strange furry creature standing stock still in the trees ahead. I knew that if I showed fear it might attack me, so I stayed where I was.

The creature raised its arm. I gripped my ax.

It reached up to its head and pulled on the fur, revealing the head and face of a girl! Around her neck was a red scarf.

She stepped slowly toward me on snowshoes, and I saw that she was a good head shorter than I was. She had seemed so much bigger in the woods. I was no longer afraid, but curious. Her glossy black hair was braided to one side in a single plait, and her red scarf matched the thread I had found on the tree.

We stood staring at each other for many minutes. Her skin was honey-toned and her eyes coffee-colored. The only other women I've seen up here are the guards' wives, with their pale pink-blotched skin and colorless hair. This girl looked nothing like them. Perhaps she was one of the Cree who were banished from here to make room for a prison camp.

She was so close that I could see the challenge in her eyes and perhaps a little anger. Her breath puffed out like wisps of smoke. She wore a coat and pants woven from narrow strips of brown and gray fur, and her store-bought boots went almost to her knees. The snowshoes strapped securely to her boots seemed handmade. Although I envied her warm and durable clothes, I had a bad feeling in the pit of my stomach. Her garb was made of wild-animal fur—rabbit and fox and who knew what all else. I noticed a wide leather strap across her chest from her waist to her shoulder. She kept a rifle slung over her back, but she didn't reach for it; I decided that it was a sign that she wouldn't hurt me. Not for the moment, anyway.

I wanted to tell her I meant no harm, so I bowed slightly and said, "Good morning, young lady."

Wide-eyed, she opened her mouth as if to say something, closed it again, then dashed away as quickly as her snowshoes would allow.

After she vanished, I didn't have the heart to cut down the trees in that area. I retraced my steps and joined my fellow prisoners.

I couldn't get that girl out of my mind.

March 1915

We don't work on Sundays, so this relative freedom is something to look forward to each week. It gives us time to mend our clothing, chat, visit friends in the hospital, or get supplies from the camp store. I often read the bits of newspaper that I've stuffed in my boots. There is a church, but it's just for the military and their family. For the internees, there is a YMCA building where we can read or relax. Some of the men have begun various art projects, making things they might be able to barter for food. For example, Bohdan is building a tiny ship inside of a bottle and Yousef is doing an oil painting of the internment camp on a slab of wood, but I mostly like to sit and write, although sometimes I'll play cards. Occasionally, a priest, who travels from camp to camp, conducts religious services for the Ukrainian and Christian prisoners at the YMCA. They wouldn't be able to get in a dede for us even if they wanted to, because as far as I know, there are none in Canada. But does it really matter? In Turkey, we don't need a building to pray and in Canada we don't need a dede. God is all around us and inside of me, so all I need is a quiet place for contemplation.

I do miss dancing the semah, though, Zeynep. The last one I danced was nearly two years ago, and it was with you.

When the Ukrainian prisoners learned that the priest was visiting this week, they were excited. Curious, I decided to accompany Bohdan to see whether the service would be much different from the ones the Protestant missionaries conducted for us back home.

We arrived early and stood at the back of the YMCA's main room. At the front, a sort of portable wooden gate had been set up, which Bohdan explained was to represent the gates to heaven. Behind the gate was a long table covered with heavily embroidered linen. In the center was an ornate golden cross, candles, and a golden cup—all much fancier than what the Protestants use.

There were no chairs put out, so I asked Bohdan where we would sit and he just smiled, telling me that we'd be standing for the whole hour—another difference between the Ukrainians and the Protestants.

The priest didn't bring an organ either. You know how those Protestant missionaries drag those rickety things in wagons though mud and over mountains just to make sure there's music to accompany the singing? Bohdan looked at me like I was crazy when I asked where the organ was. He said that only human voices could properly praise God. The sentiment seems right, but I can't imagine dancing the semah without the accompaniment of the bağlama.

As we stood there, prisoners entered in groups of twos and threes, and pretty soon almost the entire room was filled. Just before the service was supposed to start, the girl from the woods brushed slowly past me, not seeming to see me there at all. I thought it was curious that she would attend the prisoners' religious service, but maybe she wasn't allowed in the church either. Her red scarf was loosely draped over the top of her head like a veil, but her long, black braid hung down her back. Her rabbit-skin coat was replaced with a long gingham skirt and a leather vest tooled with porcupine quills and beads. She walked to the front row and stood, her head held high. A ripple of whispers, elbows nudging, fingers pointing. She was the only female in the room.

Tomas, one of the internees and a bit of a troublemaker, edged his way from the back of the room until he was just behind her. The priest came in and was about to start when I noticed Tomas reach out and tug the girl's long braid. She pretended not to notice.

I didn't want to disrupt the service, Zeynep, but I wasn't about to watch Tomas bother the girl. I thought of you, all alone with no one to look after you. How would I feel if no one came to your defense? By helping her, it was like helping you. I nudged Bohdan, and pointed to what was happening. The two of us walked up the middle aisle and slipped in behind the girl, one of us on either side of Tomas. He kept his hands on a prayer book for the rest of the service.

The priest did the entire liturgy in Ukrainian, so I didn't understand a word of it, but it was quite interesting to watch how these people worshipped God. They chanted and made symbols in the air with their hands that reminded me of three crosses. They sang surprisingly well, keeping in time with each other even though they had no musical instruments to help them along. I guess they were used to it. The girl from the woods did not sing.

Tomas left quickly after the service. The girl turned around and smiled at us both. "Thank you for making that man stop pulling my hair," she said, holding out her hand. "My name is Nadie."

"My name is Ali, and this is my friend Bohdan," I said. "It is a pleasure to meet you."

"I'm sure we'll see each other again," said Nadie. She turned and spoke to the priest, then walked out. The priest came to talk to us for a little bit and then he left too. We walked out and I looked all over to see if I could catch another glimpse of Nadie, but she had vanished.

Late March 1915

If we had come to Canada together, Zeynep, where would you be now? None of the people interned here are women. Bohdan's wife is in Alberta trying to run a 160-acre farm on her own. At least she is in the country and should have some food, but if you had come with me, we would have been living in the city together. You would have been fired from your job just like I was, but you wouldn't have been interned. Does that mean if you had come with me, you'd be starving on the street right now?

I still regret leaving you behind, but I don't know what the answer is. This war must end soon so I can find you. Otherwise I'll go mad with worry.

Fatma and the children have been on my mind of late. Yousef is tired and sullen. It is torture for him now that Fatma's letters cannot get through and he has no idea whether they are affected by the war.

I try not to think about the bad things that may be happening to you, Zeynep. I like to remember you as you were: in the village, safe and secure, surrounded by family. If you were there, you could help Fatma and the children. You could go up to the mountains in the summer, eat berries, pick flowers, and tend the sheep and goats. But you're not there. I have trouble fixing an image of you in my mind that does not terrify me. Whenever I try, I see you on the street, trampled, covered with blood. I must banish these thoughts or I will go mad. How I wish this war would end. When it does, will you forgive me? Will you keep yourself safe and will we see each other again?

I take that back.

Even if we never see each other again, I want you to be safe. And happy. Whether we're destined to be together is not the point. What I'm trying to say is that I love you, Zeynep, and even if you no longer love me, I still want you to be happy. Not trampled in the street and covered with blood.

We are supposed to be paid twenty-five cents a day for our work here, but we're not actually given that money in cash. Instead, the amount is written in a ledger at the camp store, where we can buy small luxuries to break the monotony of our plain diet: tea, coffee, and sugar, and also craft supplies like paint, glue, and brushes The amount is deducted from our account. The prices they charge us are higher than what they charge the soldiers. This is unfair, of course, but what can we do about it? We are their prisoners and we're at their mercy.

After this, I could no longer write in my journal for Zeynep. It would hurt her to know more about Nadie and what happened next.

It was Sunday and the first day of spring. The temperature hovered around freezing, but the sun was bright. I was in the camp store to buy some sugar when I became distracted by the wonderful items that only the camp guards and their wives could afford: knitted socks and scarves, imported biscuits, hard candies, chocolates, and cigars. Just then, Nadie came in, alone as always, wearing her beaded vest and gingham skirt, and the red scarf looped loosely around her shoulders. She looked like a girl instead of a wild creature, and that's not necessarily a good thing at an internment camp filled with lonely men. And of course Tomas had to be in the store right then buying cigarettes. He let out a low whistle when he noticed her; I was outraged on her behalf. It made me think of Zeynep, all alone. The thought of strange men bothering her made my blood boil.

Nadie pretended not to hear Tomas and she kept her eyes focused on the floor, but I saw her blush with embarrassment. She walked up to the counter and said to Private Michael Harrington, the store clerk, "I have pelts on my travois outside. Can I bring them in for trade?"

Now I understood why I had seen her in the woods. Hunting animals for their fur was the way she made her living, which shocked me. It was sinful that the soldiers made us cut down trees to make prisons. But this girl, who seemed so nice and innocent, of her own free will killed God's animals for the value of their pelts. I knew that she was not a bad person, but what she was doing seemed utterly wrong to me. Then again, her religion was different from mine. Maybe in Cree culture, this was fine. It roused my curiosity about her beliefs.

"A pretty little thing like you tracking game?" Private Harrington said, looking her up and down. "Sure. Show me what you've got."

Tomas chortled.

Harrington was a soldier. Why was he being so rude to Nadie? She walked out and I stepped out behind her. Her travois was a wooden A-frame platform lashed together with thin willow branches. Piled on top of it were a couple of heavy-looking flat-tied sacks. Nadie put her arms under one of the sacks, and with a grunt, lifted it up.

"Let me help you," I said. Lifting up the remaining sack of pelts, I imagined a stack of corpses. A single sack was surprisingly heavy, and she had dragged them both on this simple travois? How far had she traveled? I followed her into the store and set my sack on the counter beside the one that she had brought in, then continued with my shopping.

Harrington opened up the bag. I looked over the shelf in order to see the variety of lush and silky pelts. All those poor dead animals.

"These are not very fine quality," he ventured, but his tone belied the words.

"Put your hand on this and feel how soft it is," said Nadie, pulling out a particularly thick fur the color of pale honey. "This is lynx."

Harrington ran his hand over the lynx pelt. His eyes widened slightly, but he only said, "What else do you have?"

"Mostly beaver, but there's marten as well," she said, folding a few of the pelts over until she got to a velvety brown one.

As I watched the two haggle, my curiosity about Nadie increased. This girl was all alone in the woods yet she managed to set traps for beaver and marten, catch them, skin them, and cure the fur? I didn't want to think about how she managed to kill the lynx.

"I suppose I can take them all," said Harrington.

He tried to bargain Nadie down, but she held firm. "If you don't pay me fairly for these, I'll take them elsewhere."

"There's no other store for miles," said Harrington.

"Then I will carry them for miles."

I imagined Nadie dragging that heavy travois through the snow for miles on end. How did she do it?

The clerk relented. He counted out the furs and they agreed on a price. Nadie went through the store and came back with just a few items: coffee, sugar, and a tin of cookies. "The rest I want in cash," she said.

Nadie tucked the money away and picked up her items. She walked toward the door. Tomas had been watching as intently as I had. He hurried over to her and grabbed the coffee tin out of her hands.

"I'll carry it for you," he said.

I shook my head at the absurdity of it all. This girl had trapped and skinned all those animals on her own, then dragged the pelts all this way on her handmade travois—and Tomas thought she needed help carrying out a tin of coffee?

"Please," said Nadie. "I can carry this by myself."

"I'll give it back if you give me a kiss," said Tomas.

His insolence enraged me. I strode over and grabbed his arm. "Leave the girl alone."

"Why?" he said. "So you can have your way with her?"

I punched Tomas hard in the gut, then kept on pounding him. He belted me in the face, bloodying my lip. Nadie fled.

Harrington pulled me off Tomas and pinned me to the wall. Tomas, not much the worse for wear, ran out and brought back Officer Wilkin. Between the clerk's story and Tomas's version, I came off looking like the bad guy.

"Ali, I'm surprised at you," said Officer Wilkin. "I had chalked you up as a more peaceable sort."

I was not about to give Tomas the satisfaction of hearing me defend myself. I knew that between him and the clerk, anything I said would be refuted. I stood there silently, feeling the warmth of blood trickling down my chin, ready to take my punishment.

"You give me no choice," said Wilkin. "A week on Prison Island. We can't have fist fights."

Tomas had been looking uninjured up to this point, but I guess he figured it was time for some theatrics. He clutched onto the edge of the counter and pretended to be in pain. "I think I'm going to be sick," he whined.

"I'll get him to the hospital, sir," said Harrington.

"Very good," the officer said, turning to me. "Ali, you've got ten minutes to get into warmer clothing. I'll be sending guards to escort you to Prison Island.

Privates McPhee and Donaldson, who escorted me, seemed friendly enough despite their job. They were not rough with me or unkind, just businesslike.

I walked between them down to the small wooden pier at the edge of the river. A rowboat sat on the pier, crusted with ice.

They rocked the boat back and forth until it came loose, and then pushed it into the water.

McPhee stepped in and sat on a plank at the stern. He gestured for me to follow. I got in gingerly, clutching my six blankets and feeling the whole boat wobble back and forth until I settled down. Donaldson nudged the boat farther into the water, then stepped in himself and sat at the bow. "Prisoners row themselves," he said, pointing to an oar on either side of the boat, attached with metal rings. Back home we used a raft and a long pole to cross a river. I have never rowed a boat before, so I felt nervous doing it for the first time in a cold river with chunks of ice swirling past. With some prompting from the guards, I got the hang of it and pretty soon we arrived at Prison Island. McPhee stepped out onto the icy beach, then steadied the boat so Donaldson and I could get out. From this vantage point I could see that one of the sentry stations at the camp had a clear view of the island.

"This way," said McPhee, leading me into the trees.

The small wood cabin was the size of a jail cell. It had been a mild day, but with the cold wind from the river and the shading from the surrounding trees, the cabin interior felt exceedingly cold. There was nothing in the room but a bare wooden cot and two pails. McPhee handed me a large loaf of bread while Donaldson went down to the river's edge to fill one of the pails with water.

"You're lucky," Donaldson said as he returned the pail to my cell. "Usually these military confinement units are built under the ground, but it hasn't thawed since we got here, so you're above ground."

It was a small mercy.

"The empty pail is your toilet," McPhee said. "Don't get the two mixed up." He laughed at his feeble joke.

I sat down on the bare wooden cot and the guards left, bolting the door from the outside. They walked away and I could hear drifts of their conversation, then the water splashing as they got back into the boat.

Silence.

I stood up and unfolded the blankets, wrapping them around myself for maximum warmth. I sat back down on the edge of the cot, stunned by my circumstances. I have always tried to live my life honorably, and standing up for Nadie was the right thing to do. If I had to do it all over again, would I still fight Tomas? Of course. I couldn't imagine standing there and letting him abuse that girl. Just thinking about it made me angry again. I could only hope that someone would stand up for Zeynep's honor if need be. Even though Officer Wilkin assumed I was in the wrong, I knew in my heart that I had done the right thing. As I thought about my current circumstances, I felt a mixture of rage and fear. What else could possibly happen to me? I had been fired for no good reason—simply because the country I had fled was now at war with Canada. And I had been arrested for no good reason—on a trumped-up charge that all of us from Turkey had planned to blow up a post office. Had we been imprisoned in Brantford or even Toronto, it wouldn't have been so bad, but instead we were taken to this frozen wilderness.

And the soldiers burned our belongings: my money, my letters, my photograph of Zeynep all going up in flames. The money I could earn again, although it might take years, but the precious letters and the irreplaceable photograph? That was the worst punishment of all.

Sitting in the cold, dark prison with nothing to do and no one to talk to terrified me. As I sat there, shivering and alone, I wondered when the guards would come back. Yes, this was solitary confinement, but surely they'd check up on me every once in a while over the week? I looked down at my one loaf of bread and the one pail of water. How long was that supposed to last? Surely they'd come back with more each day? There was no window in my prison, but I watched the thin strip of light seep through the cracks between the logs. Gradually, all of the light disappeared. I tightened the blankets around my shoulders and lay down on the cot.

The dark solitude gave my mind the freedom to wander. I willed myself back home, back to Zeynep's side; to our rock at the foot of the mountains, the warmth of the sun on our shoulders as we gazed down on our village. I reached out and clasped one of Zeynep's hands in mine and brought it to my lips. One by one I kissed each of her fingertips. "I never meant to leave you, Zeynep," I said. "Please forgive me."

She said nothing, and didn't turn to look at me, but kept regarding our village in silence.

I ran my palm over her lush, dark braid, pausing for a moment at the red strip of cloth that fastened it. I caressed the side of her face until my fingertips were under her chin then turned her face to me.

It was not Zeynep but Nadie who looked searchingly into my eyes.

I jolted up from the cot, trying to get my bearings. My heart filled with guilt for dreaming of Nadie instead of Zeynep. Why had my imagination done that?

Time loses its meaning when you're imprisoned in complete isolation, and my intermingled thoughts of Zeynep and Nadie made me frightened to fall asleep. I got up and paced.

Sounds filtered in from outside, but in the absence of visuals my imagination transformed them into sinister beings. A scratching on the wood outside—was that the bough of a spruce on my prison as it blew in the wind or a moose scraping its antlers against the side of the cabin? Or maybe a black bear awakened early from its winter slumber could smell me through the cracks and break down my wooden prison and eat me alive.

I broke my bread into seven pieces, ate one of them, then kept on pacing. After a while, the faint strips of light reappeared through the cracks. It must be day two. I pushed my thumbnail into a soft spot in the wood and tried to make a faint X. I ate another piece of bread.

That night I dreamed of being back home in the stone-and-clay hut where I was born. Me, Mama, Yousef, our sleeping rugs and pillows clustered around the brazier. Soft sighing sounds of rhythmic breathing, the faint scent of last night's repast of dried apricots, figs, and pine nuts, shared as we told family stories.

Cozy. Safe. I wanted to wake up and find Zeynep. We could go to our rock in the mountains. I would wrap my arms around her and never let her go. Then I opened my eyes and the dream evaporated. I was back in the cold lonely cabin—banished here for standing up for someone weaker than me. Everyone and everything I loved was gone.

I stood up and stomped my feet to warm them, then began pacing the length of the tiny cabin. I would not give up. I was determined to live my life with dignity no matter what.

For each day that I thought had passed, I ate one of the pieces of bread and pressed my fingernail into the soft wood to make another X. I had just finished the seventh piece when a scraping sound of metal on metal made my heart race. The door opened and the light nearly blinded me. The gust of fresh air made me shiver, but it was also cleansing. For days I had been surrounded by the stink of my own excrement in the pail. I shielded my eyes with my hands and squinted at the silhouette in front of me.

"Am I going back to the camp now?" I asked.

A hearty chuckle. Private McPhee. "You've only been locked up three days. Boy, does it smell in here. You'll think twice before getting into any more fights."

He set another loaf of bread on my cot and refilled my drinking pail, leaving the door open to air out my cell as he did so. Even though it was bone chilling outside, it was a relief to breathe fresh air again. He picked up my pail and unceremoniously dumped the contents in the bushes. He returned with it empty but still foul-smelling.

"Four more days. Make this bread and water last," he said, closing the door behind him. I listened to the bolt clunk into place and the oar splashing the water before I let out a wail. Could I last another four days? Did I have a choice? I broke my loaf into four pieces then slowly chewed on one of them.

My sense of time was entirely fractured. Hadn't I carefully marked each change from daylight to dark with an X? How could I have got it so wrong? But then again, how much sunlight could filter down to me in the deep woods? Perhaps the changing light and dark through the cracks was my imagination working overtime.

I heard the door scrape open again. But surely it wasn't four days? It seemed like only minutes since McPhee had left. Again I thought of a black bear waking up early from hibernation. Back home there were bears on the mountain, but they stayed away from people. Had a Canadian bear figured out how to open a bolt? Was my punishment now to be devoured by one of those wild creatures?

The door yawned open. Cold, fresh air gusted in. A slight figure silhouetted against the twilight: Not some monster, but a girl.

Once I got over my shock, I felt a rush of embarrassment. What must she think of me? And who was she? The daughter or wife of one of the soldiers? As my eyes adjusted, I saw that she wore a familiar coat of woven fur—Nadie.

She stepped inside, leaving the door open so light and air could filter in. The thought of us being in this cell alone together terrified me.

"I'm sorry," she said. "It's my fault you're being punished. Let me get you out of here."

Of all the things she could have said, that's not what I had expected.

"If I leave this cabin, they'll only hunt me down and capture me. Then they'll put me in a worse place for a longer time."

"But you can hide."

"Others have tried, but they all come back, frostbitten and starved. Or they're brought back, dead."

"Those men didn't have help," she said. "Do I look frostbitten or starved or dead?"

The kindness I did for her was small, what any honorable man would do if he saw a woman insulted. And for that small kindness she was offering me my freedom and refuge. The magnitude of her generosity left me speechless.

"The sooner we leave, the safer you'll be."

If I went with her, I would leave behind my brother Yousef, the only family I had left. I would never return to my old way of life when the war ended. I would be an escapee. But what did I have to go back to? Zeynep was lost to me. And Yousef could manage on his own.

Nadie walked over and clenched my hand in a firm grip. "We leave now."

I was already fully dressed, right down to my coat and boots. I wrapped one of my blankets around my shoulders like a shawl and followed her to the door.

One sentry had a clear view of the island—that I knew. But

I hoped that the trees would conceal my exit from the cabin. I left the door open. Why make the person who was punished after me suffer in that smell? A good airing out would be a kindness.

"This way," said Nadie.

The ground around the cabin was mostly ice broken up with patches of mud and snow, which I stepped around to avoid sinking in the soft muck. I gazed up into the sky and nearly wept—the cabin, Nadie, my shivers—they all disappeared. Above me was the moon at its fullest and stars that hung like jewels on velvet. I raised my arms to the universe and Allah, and gave a prayer of thanks. A rush of memories: praying under this selfsame moon with Zeynep at my side, dancing the semah with Zeynep and my friends and family, bidding my mother goodbye. My mountains, my village, my Zeynep.

"Ali, it's time."

Nadie broke the spell. I looked around and was back in the present. She led me to a spot that was not visible from the camp. A narrow watercraft was tied to a tree at the edge of the lapping water.

"Step into the canoe and move to the far end," she said.

Once I was in, Nadie pushed the canoe out into the icy river, then gracefully jumped in just before the currents caught it and dragged it away from the island. I gripped the birch-bark sides and tried to ignore my nerves. The canoe felt precariously tipsy and I imagined us both plunging to our deaths in the black depths—but more than that—where was she taking me?

"Think of your spine as a willow tree, said Nadie. "Let your body move with the water." She reached into the middle of the canoe and pulled out a double-ended paddle. She positioned herself at the opposite end of the craft and expertly guided it through the dark.

"If you get tired, I can take a turn," I said.

"Not necessary," she said, her smile bright in the twilight. "I know this river like I know my own heart."

Nadie maneuvered the canoe along the side of the island unseen by the internment camp, but as we neared the end of the island, she whispered, "Carefully slide down into the canoe, so they can't see you."

Easier said than done. I felt queasy and afraid of upending it, but the alternative was worse. I lay down as flat as I could and tried to let my body move in time with the lapping water and the canoe. I breathed slowly, thankful that twilight had given way to full darkness.

As we glided past the camp, I watched the moon and stars, and listened to Nadie's breathing and the rhythmic dip of the paddle in the icy water.

"You can sit up now, Ali."

I looked around in wonder. We were in the middle of the wide Kapuskasing River, surrounded by darkness broken only by the diamond-like reflections of the moon and the stars. I felt one with the universe. *Dear God, I am your servant.* I thought of my spine as a willow and trusted that Nadie knew what she was doing. I was too filled with anticipation to be bothered by the cold, but Nadie handed me a rabbit-fur blanket. It seemed wrong to touch it, as rabbits are sacred. How could I cover myself in their corpses? Why hadn't I thought to bring my own blankets? A deep shiver ran through me and I pulled the fur around my shoulders. "Thank you, God, for this gift," I prayed under my breath.

We traveled north for what seemed like hours, which gave me time to think about the audacious thing I was doing. My old life was over and Zeynep was lost to me; that was something that I was struggling to accept. This was my chance to leave the past behind. A chance to be happy.

Nadie guided the canoe to a spot on the shore on the opposite side from the internment camp. To me, the landing area looked just the same as everywhere else: an ice-glazed sandy shore covered with an awning of spruce and brush.

"How far away are we from the prison camp?" I asked her.

"About four miles—well beyond the distance they'd think to look for you." She hopped out and steadied her end of the canoe. I climbed out, feeling happy to be on solid land.

Nadie pulled the canoe completely out of the water and hid it within the bushes. "Watch your step," she said. "It's slippery here."

Branches whipped my face and I stumbled more than once. Wherever Nadie was taking me, it was well hidden. The ground changed from icy sand to mostly pristine snow. The trees grew so close together that their roots seemed intertwined. This was a part of the forest that we hadn't been sent to cut down. Yet.

"We're here."

I looked around, but in the darkness all I saw was the same vista of trees and snow. But I detected a faint smoky scent in the air and I followed it with my nose, and that's when I noticed a hole in the top of a snowdrift. I pointed to it. "Is this your home?"

Nadie smiled. "The entire forest is my home, but this is my temporary hunting pit. I'll be breaking camp soon and moving north to meet my clan for the spring feast. Come inside and let's get warm."

She led me to the camouflaged entryway through brush around the back. When I crawled in, I was enveloped in humid warmth that smelled of berries and smoked meat. It was dark except for the bit of moonlight that shone through the hole in the ceiling. Nadie came in after me and, before doing anything else, she crawled to the middle of the room and knelt by the mound of sticks in the hearth below the ceiling hole. She cradled her hands around it and gently blew, coaxing embers into a fire. She added bits of kindling and once the flames licked up, she added larger pieces of wood. The firelight illuminated the room and bunches of onions, herbs, dried fish, and rabbits that hung from the ceiling.

My heart lurched with sorrow at the sight of dead animals. How could this seemingly gentle and compassionate person be so cruel?

I removed my boots and set them by the entrance, then took off my coat for the first time in days. The fire's warmth washed over me like a healing salve. As I crawled closer to the flames, I realized that the floor was carpeted with furs. Other pelts were rolled in bundles to use as pillows. I was surrounded by corpses. All these wild animals gave up their lives so Nadie could stay warm. This girl's attitude toward wildlife seemed a contradiction to her personality, but I didn't want to prejudge. Obviously there was something I didn't understand. I settled in and almost against my will enjoyed the soft warmth. As my eyes adjusted to the firelight, I marveled at how much this room resembled my home where I grew up. Instead of furs, we used carpets and cushions, and instead of an open fire, we had the glow of a brazier. If I closed my eyes I could imagine myself as a child, with Yousef on the cushion at my side, and Mama nestled with us, telling us stories passed down through generations.

Nadie removed her own boots and coat. Underneath the fur, Nadie wore a thin cloth shirt that reached almost to her knees and covered her from neck to wrist, yet betrayed the full shape of her breasts and the narrowness of her waist. She stepped out of her fur leggings to reveal knitted long johns that clung to her skin as if her legs had been painted pale gray. Without seeming to sense my watching her, she wrapped a long gingham skirt around her hips and tied it at the waist. She sat beside me, tucking her feet under her skirt. I was intensely aware of her closeness and I could feel myself blushing.

"You must be hungry," Nadie said, her eyes soft.

She reached up and untied one of the dried fish hanging from the ceiling. She peeled back the skin and scooped out a piece of meat, then offered it to me.

I took a small piece and held it in my hand. This flesh was from a wild animal too and belonged to God, but I was Nadie's guest. I offered silent thanks to God for the food I put in my mouth. Smoky, intense, and flavorful. Much as I didn't want to enjoy this wild food, my stomach grumbled for more. Nadie pulled off another piece of fish and ate it herself, then gave me another morsel with some of the skin. Soon all that remained was the skeleton. She chewed on the larger bones until all that was left were the sharp little ones. She sucked each one carefully, making sure no flesh remained, then threw the bones on the fire. As she did, she whispered something under her breath. Perhaps thanking her god for this food, just as I had done.

"Would you like some rabbit?" she asked, reaching up to untie one of the corpses.

"I couldn't," I said hastily.

"You're not still hungry?"

"Rabbits are sacred. I could never eat one."

Nadie looked at me, her eyebrows furrowed. "They are sacred in my culture too. So are the fish."

"Then why eat the fish? Why skin the rabbits for their fur and eat their flesh?"

"We are one with nature," she said. "We take what we need to survive, but no more. And we do not waste. That's why I ate every morsel of the fish. And the rabbits? Their bones are transformed into instruments. The words I whispered after finishing the fish? I was thanking the fish for giving me strength."

Her explanation surprised me, but it also made sense. We

Alevis also did not waste and we too are one with nature. When we kill a cow or goat, every part of it is used. The hide is transformed into leather for shoes and coats, the bladder into a ball for the children, the meat into food. To waste any part would offend God. The difference was that in our culture, we only killed the animals we raised, never wildlife. Perhaps Nadie's people considered all animal life in the forest as livestock.

"What I cannot understand," said Nadie, "is how you can destroy all those trees. Surely your guards don't need so much wood?"

Her comment surprised me. "I hate cutting the trees," I told her. "Each time one falls, I feel like I've committed murder."

Nadie was quiet at this comment. I watched the reflection of the fire in her eyes. "The red thread on the tree," she said. "I put it there for you to find."

"Why?"

"That tree is my favorite. It's the oldest in that part of the woods. I hoped you wouldn't cut it down. I was watching you from a distance."

A flush of embarrassment coursed through me.

"The other prisoner teams," she said. "They don't like to cut down the trees because it's work. For you and your team, it's because of the trees."

She was exactly right. And she was the first non-Alevi I had ever met who seemed to understand. Our cultures were vastly different yet we had so much in common.

We sat side by side, wordlessly watching the fire. The long night stretched out before us.

Nadie and I were in the middle of the wilderness, completely on our own, and I was halfway around the world from home. Why had Nadie brought me here? What did she expect from me?

"You've been living here all on your own for the entire winter?" I asked.

"Not all on my own," replied Nadie. "There are other trappers scattered here and there throughout forest and along the river. Usually there would be more of us in the pit, but I was dared to do this."

"Someone dared you to trap on your own?"

"I've lived at the church school these past few years," said Nadie. "My father claimed that I've turned into a white woman, what with praying in church and wearing gingham skirts, reading English books. I told him he was wrong, that I would never forget who I was. He dared me to prove it. So I did. Instead of going in a group camp, I came out here on my own. And I've done well. My father will be proud when he sees the money my pelts brought in."

I thought of that stack of bills Harrington had handed over to her for the furs. It reminded me of my hard-earned savings from the foundry and how it had gone up in flames, turning my hopes and dreams to ash. Nadie had worked hard for her savings.

"What will you do with that money?" I asked.

"I'm going south," she said. "On the train to Toronto. I want to go to school."

"But you've already been to the church school."

"They can only teach me so much." Nadie reached over and undid one of the rolled-up pelts. Cookies—the same tin that she had bought at the camp store. She opened the lid, took out two, and handed one to me.

"My mother died from an infection," said Nadie. "That's why I want to go to school."

"And do what?"

"Become a healer. I already know traditional methods. My grandmother taught me. Now I want to learn more. Once I do, I'll go back home and help my people."

"Will you have enough money for that?"

"I don't know."

"Will the white people let you into their school?"

"I don't know, but I'm going to try."

Nadie's dream was firm, but I wondered if she'd ever achieve it. In my community, men and women were equal, but it wasn't like that in the rest of Turkey. In Canada, the men were in charge—and rich, white men at that. Nadie's talk of the future made me realize that she didn't really see me as a part of it.

"And what will I do when you go south?" I asked her.

Nadie looked up at me and smiled. "I know my clan will welcome you. My father will teach you how to hunt and fish and live in the bush. You'll be free."

I stared at the cookie, small and pale with a sprinkling of sugar. To have a family again would be truly wonderful. I felt more at home with Nadie than with anyone else in Canada, and I was sure her family would be just as welcoming, but could I spend my life hunting? It went against all of my beliefs.

I bit the cookie and slowly chewed, willing it to help me decide. The soldiers buy these cookies, but I had never tasted one before. A tin costs twenty-five cents, a day's wages in the prison camp. I took another bite and felt a twinge of sorrow as I remembered a cookie I had bought for Zeynep at Petrosian's long ago. Would I really never see her again?

"Vanilla," Nadie said, oblivious to my inner turmoil. She bit the edge of hers and chewed like a mouse. "We had these same cookies at school, but not often. The teachers usually kept them for themselves."

"In Anatolia, where I come from, we had church schools too."

"Did you have these cookies?"

I smiled. "No. But we had the missionaries' clinics and schools, and of course their churches."

"Is that why you went to church?" she asked.

"I only went that one time," I told her. "I was curious to see if it would be different from the Christian services back home. Why do you go to the internees' church service?"

"I wanted to see what the Ukrainian religion was like. It's not that much different from other Christian churches."

"Do you believe in their God?"

"There is only one Great Spirit," said Nadie. "We call him Kitchi Manitou. They call him God."

"I call him Jesus, Allah, Muhammad, or God," I told her. "But he isn't in a church or a building and he doesn't care if we pray to him. God is everywhere and is part of every human, everything in the universe. He judges us by our deeds, whether we treat others the way we'd like to be treated."

Nadie looked at me strangely. "That's the same as Kitchi Manitou." She took another bite of her cookie and chewed slowly. "Why did you help me in the store?"

"Why wouldn't I help you?" I asked her. "Anyone would have done the same."

She shook her head. "That's not true," she said. "I think it's because of your Great Spirit."

We talked for hours about our beliefs and culture, and it amazed me how much was the same. Nadie told me about how the native people had lived here for thousands of years before the Europeans came. I told her that it was the same for us in Anatolia. Our ancestors had lived there, practicing our religion before Christianity or Islam even existed. I told her about our semah.

"It sounds like the Plains Cree round dance," she said. "Can you show me?"

I was thoroughly warmed by the fire, so I pulled on my boots but left my coat, hat, and gloves inside. Nadie did the same.

"This way," she said, tugging me by the hand.

She led me to a clearing a few dozen feet away from the hunting pit. There was an unobstructed view of moon and stars above. "This is perfect," I said. "Face me, and do as I do."

I stood rigid with my arms at my side and looked up to the moon. Nadie did the same about a few feet in front of me. I began to sing one of our holy songs about a traveler just loud enough so Nadie could hear the rhythm, then raised my arms and danced the steps in a clockwise circle to mimic the planets orbiting the sun. Normally, the circle would have been larger and have more people. Nadie got the rhythm right away and mirrored my steps. I added in the spins. She laughed and spun as well.

We spun and danced for an hour or more. I was entranced. Nadie disappeared and I had gone back in time, dancing with Zeynep again, my mother, my friends back home. My heart was filled with bittersweet joy.

Then we stopped dancing and stood there, panting with exhaustion under the moonlight.

"Let me teach you the round dance," she said. "I only did it once as a child when we visited family in the West, but I'll never forget the steps."

She pushed me away and we stood a few feet apart again. "There would normally be a drummer to help us keep time," she said. "The beat is like this." She clapped her hands in a rhythm similar to a heartbeat. When she sang, her face lit up as if it were someone else inside of her body. The words and the rhythm were wild but structured. I couldn't sing with her, but I copied her steps. We danced a few feet apart, but it was as if we were tied together. She danced, in a slow circle clockwise like in the semah, but we stayed facing each other instead of twirling.

I stared into Nadie's dark brown eyes as we danced, and the world disappeared. Her eyes, lips, nose, and nothing more.

Suddenly, Nadie stopped. I was soaked with sweat and chilled by the night.

"Let's go inside," I said.

The fire had nearly gone out. Nadie's teeth chattered as she coaxed the embers back into a flame. I wrapped a fur around her shoulders. "Let me get you warm," I said. We snuggled under the furs and I could feel Nadie's body pressed close to mine.

"We should sleep now," she said, resting her head on my shoulder.

As we lay there, I stared at the rabbits and fish hanging from the ceiling, overwhelmed at the sudden change my life had taken. I was free, safe, and had a future. But did I really want to abandon my past and join Nadie's clan? What of Zeynep? Even if we were destined to be apart, could I abandon who I was?

Would Nadie's community accept me or would I be their guest for just a short time, then be banished to the wilderness, living alone? I gently shifted my shoulder under Nadie's head and as I turned, Zeynep's evil-eye pendant fell out of my shirt and landed on Nadie's cheek. She didn't wake up. I held the stone to my face, watching it catch the light from the fire, glittering orange and green and blue. *Zeynep, where is she? Will I ever see her again?*

I thought of Nadie's determination to go to school despite the odds. It was important never to give up. I could learn from Nadie.

And that's when it became clear to me: I could not stay. Letting Nadie rescue me was the easy way out. I had to stand up for myself. I had to return to the cabin on Prison Island.

As an escapee, I would never be allowed to be a Canadian citizen. And if I wasn't a citizen, how could I bring Zeynep here? If I didn't take my punishment like a man, Zeynep was lost to me forever. If she was lost to me already, I could take comfort in knowing that I did everything in my power to bring us together.

I brushed a lock of hair away from Nadie's face and touched my lips to her brow.

I awoke to sunlight beaming down through the hole in the ceiling and Nadie kneeling across from me, methodically packing away her items from the hunting pit. When she looked over and saw that I was awake, she smiled. "Time to get up," she said. "We should be leaving soon."

I sat up and stretched, then felt very awkward. "I can't go back with you."

"What do you mean?"

"I need to get back to the camp," I told her. "And take my punishment."

"But I set you free," she said. "You have a new life ahead of you."

She set down the fur she had been folding and crawled over to me. She lay down and stretched her body out alongside mine. I reveled in her warmth and wrapped my arms around her waist. "You want to go to school, right?"

She turned her head and looked me in the eyes. "Yes."

"I have dreams and wishes too."

I told her about Zeynep. "You've shown me how important it is to follow your dreams."

Nadie was quiet, wrapped in her own thoughts as we cuddled under the furs. Then she sat up and looked at me, a sad smile on her face. "I'll take you back to Prison Island."

It was broad daylight as we approached the camp, so I lay down in Nadie's canoe covered with rabbit fur. I listened to her paddle dip in and out of the water and we glided past the camp and behind Prison Island. She pulled back the cover and I sat up. I helped her pull the canoe onto the shore. Together, we walked to the small cabin prison cell.

The door was bolted closed.

Hadn't I left it open? Maybe not. I opened the bolt, but before stepping inside, I turned to Nadie and wrapped my arms around her. "Will I ever see you again?"

She looked into my eyes and smiled. "Maybe," she said. "My English name is Nettie Martin. What's your full name?"

"Ali Hassan," I said. "May God watch over you."

"And Kitchi Manitou over you," she said.

I stepped inside and listened as Nadie slid the bolt into place. I walked over to the cot with my blankets. That's when I noticed the new loaf of bread sitting beside the three stale chunks from yesterday's loaf.

Someone had been here.

PART FIVE

HARPUT, ANATOLIA

May 14, 1915

Today I dressed in my old clothing, then went out to the garden and rolled around in the soil to make it look like I had been traveling. I rubbed dirt onto my face and put a red scarf over my stubble of hair. Lenore gathered together all the papers the soldiers might find suspicious: Reverend Emmonds' diary, her own personal letters, an Armenian phrase book. I put my journal on top, bundled it with clothing, and wrapped it all in an old faded kerchief.

As I walked down to Mezreh with my precious bundle, I passed a few Turkish soldiers. They didn't give me a second glance, likely thinking I was nothing more than a simple

Kurdish girl from the mountains. When I got to the American Consulate building, I recited Psalm 23:4: "Yea, though I walk through the valley of the shadow of death, I will fear no evil: for thou art with me; thy rod and thy staff they comfort me."

Lenore told me that the Christian phrase would act as a password. The Armenian guards opened the gate.

The mulberry trees blossomed with white flowers whose sweet scent enveloped me as I walked down the pathway to the mansion. A servant opened the door and ushered me in. I tried not to stare, but I had never seen a house like this one before. Fancy paper covered walls that were adorned with many lifelike portraits. It felt as if a hundred eyes were watching me. Thick Armenian rugs carpeted the floor and I noticed another hanging on the wall at the top of the stairs. A large crystal chandelier, suspended on a long chain in the middle of the room, sparkled as sunlight shone through the high windows. I was overwhelmed with the richness of it all. The servant took me to a book-lined room with a big wooden desk. I sat on the edge of one of the chairs and waited. Within minutes, the consul entered. He looked different up close compared to when I had seen him last year hiking in a khaki shirt, pants, and big boots. Now he was dressed in a black wool American suit with a tie around his neck, and his face was red from the heat. His shiny, black shoes looked uncomfortable. The little hair that he had was pure white and clipped close to his head. Maybe he'd survived typhus too?

"You're Zeynep, Lenore Emmonds' helper, correct?" he asked me.

I stumbled to my feet and bowed. "Yes, sir."

"And you're Turkish?"

"No, sir, I am an Alevi Kurd."

"You have something to leave here for safekeeping?"

I set my bundle on my chair and opened it, drawing out the stack of incriminating items. He looked through them. When he got to my journal, he opened it and frowned. "Who wrote this?"

"I did."

"This is Arabic script, but I can't read it."

"That's because it is written in Zaza," I said. "Lately I have been writing about what I've seen since the war started," I told him. "But it's not for me. My...friend...asked me to keep a journal, so when we're back together he can read about what I did while we were apart. He's making a journal for me as well."

"That's a fine idea," said the consul. "I take it your friend is working in America?"

"In Canada."

"Your journal is important," he said. "Not just for you and your friend, but for the world. I'd like you to continue writing it."

"I can't. If the soldiers catch me, our whole household could be punished."

"Could the soldiers read it?" he asked.

"Not unless they were Alevi Kurds," I said.

Consul Davis tapped the cover of my journal with his finger and said, "I'll keep this one in my safe, but I would like you to come here for a few hours each week. I'll give you sheets of paper and a safe place to write, and I'll hide the papers as you complete them. Your observations are of great value. We'll figure out a job for you, so you will have a reason to come here regularly."

My eventual job was to buy food at the market for the Consulate. Most of the consul's employees are Armenian and they can't go to the market safely, but I can. For a while, the consul had to buy his own food, but now he can do more important things. He has insisted that he pay me to do this, even though I told him no. I've asked him to hold onto my money. His safe is the most secure place in the entire region.

June 9, 1915

A pounding at the door woke me up. I quickly pulled on a skirt and blouse and ran to the door just before Yester got to the kitchen. An officer stood there, rifle in hand. Behind him stood nine soldiers. "Step aside," he said. "We're here to search the house."

By this time Reverend Emmonds was up, his shirt buttoned haphazardly and his glasses askew. "My wife is still sleeping," he said. "Can you give us a few minutes?"

The officer grunted, then walked right in, the soldiers fanning out into all the rooms. Fatma screamed from upstairs. Minutes later, she came down half-dressed, holding onto Suleyman.

We stood by helplessly as the soldiers tore up floorboards, and pulled plaster off the walls. They were very good at their job, looking in the most ingenious places, like the garden and the garbage and inside the mattresses. Thank God my journal was not here. As it was, the telephone nearly got us all killed; not the phone itself but the numbers for the other missionaries that were written beside it on the wall.

"You're sending secret messages to our enemies," shouted the officer.

"If I were sending secret messages, I would have hidden it better than that," said Lenore. "Those numbers are only the codes for the other missionaries in the area."

He pulled a knife from his belt, and for a moment I thought he was going to stab Lenore. She took one step back.

The officer cut the telephone cord and ripped the machine out of the wall. "No more talking to enemies," he said. Had she been any nationality other than American, he would have killed her on the spot.

Soldiers went down into the root cellar. I forced myself to act naturally, breathing in, breathing out, but my heart pounded so hard in my chest that I was sure the officer who remained in the kitchen could hear it. Yester went to the cupboard and took out a teapot, seemingly intent on making breakfast as usual. The soldiers were in the root cellar for a very long time.

They finally came up.

"Anything?" asked the officer. They shook their heads.

The soldiers left.

Yester dropped the teapot and her knees buckled. I caught her just before her head hit the kitchen floor.

While Yester sobbed hysterically, I went down into the root

cellar with Keghani to see if we could see what happened. Shelves of food and supplies had been pulled down to the floor. Boxes opened, flour and grain scattered about, jars smashed. The stones in front of the hiding place had been pried out. We looked inside.

Empty.

Raffi and Onnig had not been taken by the soldiers. That was certain. If they'd been caught, the soldiers would have set fire to the house with us still inside. Raffi and Onnig must have escaped through the outhouse.

"I brought them down food last night," said Keghani, frowning in confusion. "They didn't say anything about leaving."

Later that day, as I walked to the hospital with Keghani, we passed the public square. A dozen young men had been hanged, their necks broken and their bodies twisting in the wind. I searched their faces—neither Raffi nor Onnig was among them.

Keghani's eyes lit upon one of the men and she began to shake. "That's Vartan," she said. "He was in my class."

"Armenian revolutionaries," said a veiled woman as she passed by us.

Keghani raised her hand to slap the woman, but I grabbed it just in time. I wrapped my arm around her waist and we ran back home.

June 15, 1915

The sounds in the street made it difficult to sleep last night. Suleyman, however, can sleep through anything and he was snuggled up in Fatma's arms. Aunt Besee tossed and turned with her eyes closed. I lay as still as I could and listened.

The banging of soldiers going house to house, knocking on doors, shouting, "Armenian?" Chains clanking, women crying. Were they taking yet more Armenian men to the Red Konak?

When I got ready to go to the hospital, Lenore said that Keghani was staying home. "It's too dangerous for any of our Armenians to be out on the street."

I went back to the bedroom and changed into my country clothing. It would be safer if I didn't look like I worked for Christians. The streets were eerily quiet. The only people other than me who were out were soldiers. Each time I passed one, I bowed my head, mumbling, "Allah is great." Invariably, he would return the greeting and continue on his way.

The Ward Four linen cupboard is on the main floor around the back. As I approached it, I noticed a smear of blood that went down the hallway and ended beneath my door. *Perhaps a patient has helped himself to fresh linens*, I thought, but when I opened the door, I nearly tripped over Dr. Tapalian's bruised and bloodied body. I fell to my knees and put my fingers to his neck, searching for a pulse. He was alive. His scalp was a mass of mottled and bloodied spots where his magnificent dark wiry hair had been yanked out by the root.

"Dr. Tapalian," I said. "What happened to you?"

"Close the door," he whispered. "I can't let anyone find me." As he raised his hand to shield his face from the hall light, I gasped in horror. His fingernails had been torn out. I closed the door.

"You were taken by the soldiers last night?"

"Eight hundred Armenians were taken to the Red Konak and tortured—the ones they consider leaders. They want us to tell them where we've hidden bombs, but there are no bombs! They left me for dead and I managed to escape."

"I need to get you help."

"No! If word gets out that I'm here, they'll arrest me again. I need to stay hidden."

I pulled down some of the linens and made a bed for him on the floor and bandaged his fingers as best as I could.

"Can you clean the wounds on my feet?"

And that's when I learned a new word: *bastinadoed*. A form of torture. Tears welled in my eyes as I cleaned the ribbon-like cuts on the soles of his feet. As I dabbed gently with disinfectant, the shards of bone through the skin felt like broken china. How would he ever walk again? His face went rigid with pain as I covered his feet with gauze and taped them up the best I could. By the time I had finished, he was trembling all over. I covered him with a blanket and got him some water. "Try to rest," I said.

An hour later, he was gone.

June 16, 1915

Miss Anton has returned from a trip with another missionary to Diyarbakir in the southwest near the desert. She came to see Lenore. I told Yester that I would prepare the tea, so she could rest. Yester has not been herself since Onnig disappeared.

After setting the tea service on the kitchen table, I looked busy as I listened in on the conversation.

"They're in a state of terror," said Miss Anton, stirring sugar into her teacup. "The Armenians dare not go outside."

"We're not letting our Armenian staff leave the premises here either," said Lenore.

"It's different," said Miss Anton. "Much worse there. Here the soldiers just go door-to-door. In Diyarbakir, soldiers are stationed on the rooftops with orders to shoot any Armenian they see."

I ran a damp rag over the countertop, willing my hand not to shake.

"My goodness," said Lenore. "What is the army thinking? Shouldn't they be concentrating on fighting the enemy instead of their own helpless citizens?"

"The government's plan is to kill all the Armenians because they're Christian. You know that, Lenore. I wonder how long it will be before they come after us."

"They wouldn't dare come after us. We may be Christian, but they don't want to provoke the Americans into a war, and harming an American would do just that."

"On my way back here, I saw Armenians who had obviously traveled quite far on foot—women, children, even babies. They were in a terrible state: clothing in shreds and they seemed to have no food or water. They were all walking toward Diyarbakir, guided by mounted troops."

As I overheard the conversation, my mind filled with the images of those people. Did they know they were being marched to their own deaths?

Lenore held her head in her hands. "When will this madness stop?"

"It's hard to know," said Miss Anton. "It will get worse before it gets better. Now it is a criminal offense to hide Armenians." She sipped her tea. "Don't you think you should send your Armenians somewhere else to live? Otherwise you're risking your life."

I had an almost uncontrollable urge to slap Miss Anton in the face for her callousness, but I threw the dishrag into the sink instead. I did it with such force that it made a small thump. Miss Anton turned to me.

"I know you're eavesdropping," she said. "You may think I'm blunt, but you have no idea how hard this is on us."

I nodded mutely. I didn't dare trust myself to respond.

Lenore set her teacup down on the table with a clatter. "How hard it is on us? Really, Christine, I've put up with your nonsense for years, but this is the last straw. Please leave now."

Miss Anton's mouth opened but no words came out.

"And don't bother coming back."

June 23, 1915

I'm almost afraid to sleep at night. In the early hours just after dawn, I woke with a start. Again, something was going on outside. My old bedroom faces the street, so I got up quietly so I wouldn't wake Suleyman and walked down the hallway. Keghani stood silhouetted against the window.

"You heard the noises too?" I whispered.

She turned to me. "Down there. Look." Keghani wrapped her arm around my waist. By the early morning sun, we saw a winding procession of the oxcarts that used to carry garbage out of the city; now they carried men, trussed together with ropes. Beside them walked other prisoners, prodded forward by soldiers with bayonets. Ripped clothing, slashes of blood, dirt.

Keghani gasped. "Look in that cart over there," she said, pointing to one that just came into view. "Aren't those the Fabrictorian brothers?"

I squinted hard and looked where she pointed. In the cart were four men tied together and a fifth stumbling along beside them, one wrist tied to the cart. The brothers' real surname was something else, but everyone called them the Fabrictorians because they controlled many fabric businesses: carpet factories, silk mills, tailor shops, and dress boutiques. All five brothers with their wives and children lived side by side in identical houses on the best street in Mezreh, not far from the vali himself. They were rumored to be the richest family in the area.

The Fabrictorians may have been wealthy, but they were honest and people liked to work for them. The brothers also enjoyed eating, as could be seen by their round bellies and dimpled cheeks. The men below us bore the telltale signs of torture—bloodied fingertips, bare scalps, and scabs where their hair had been ripped out. The army had to be mad. If they deported the Fabrictorians, who would make their uniforms?

"You're right," I said. "And in that cart I can see Professor Medrozian."

"Those are students with him," Keghani said. "And there is the bishop."

I felt the bile rise up my throat as each cart passed. Doctors and pharmacists from our hospital were bound and bloodied. Kevork Aprahamian, a widower who owned the candy booth, was tied up in a cart with Alex Alexanian, a carpet weaver from Mezreh. And then I gasped—Dr. Tapalian. He'd been recaptured.

We watched as the procession rolled slowly out of the city and took the road to Diyarbakir. "I'm fairly sure those were the 800 men who were arrested a few days ago," I said.

Keghani turned to me, her face wet with tears. "Do you think they'll take me and Yester next?"

I thought of what Miss Anton had said and what she'd seen and I clenched my fists in anger. Could I really just stand here and watch it happen? Wasn't there some way I could help? "I'll do everything I can to protect you," I said.

"That's a nice thought," said Keghani in a flat voice.

We both left the window. Still in our nightclothes, we went downstairs to the kitchen. I was too agitated to eat. My stomach felt like it was filled with lava. I had this urge to run into the street and scream at the soldiers, but that would do no good. Right now there was only one positive thing I could do: make bandages. Keghani sat beside me. "I don't know how much more of this I can take," she said.

We sat in silence and worked, each of us wrapped in our own thoughts.

An hour, maybe two, went by...and then we heard the familiar sound of oxcarts rumbling by yet again. Were they deporting even more people? I ran upstairs to look out the big window. Empty oxcarts returning from the south. Smeared with blood, frayed rope ends blowing in the breeze. They hadn't gone far. The killing site had moved closer to us.

.   *June 26, 1915*

I was mopping the floor on Ward Four when I heard a loud bang outside the hospital. I leaned my mop against the wall and hurried outside. The streets were lined with curious people whispering among themselves, trying to guess what was going on.

Bang. Bang. Bang.

The crowd fell silent.

A small boy walked down the dusty street, banging loudly on his drum. Behind him walked the town crier, Mahmoud Havoosh. He stopped and gazed at the crowd.

"I have an important government announcement," he shouted. "Every Armenian man, woman, and child will be deported to Urfa for their safety. First are those who live in the market district. Your departure date is July 1. Please dispose of your valuables before that time. You are responsible for your own food and water."

As he listed the deportation dates for the various areas of the city, I realized that Yester and Keghani were scheduled for deportation on July 2.

My head spun with the impossibility of it all. The town crier said this was for their safety, but if that were true, why were the Armenians being singled out? Why did they have to get rid of their belongings? Urfa was in the desert. There was no food or water in the desert. Without a horse and wagon it was impossible to carry more than a few days' supply, and the army had all the horses. The trip to Urfa on foot would take a month, but most people would die of hunger or thirst or heat long before that. Would the government really go through with this?

The town crier continued up the street. The crowds around me buzzed with the news. "Finally," said one voice. "They're getting rid of the last of the infidels. The city will be cleansed." Another voice said, "This isn't right. If we kill all the Armenians, we'll bring the wrath of Allah upon ourselves."

This can't be true, I thought, imagining Keghani and Yester tied with ropes, bloodied scalps, and fingertips, in a garbage cart. I doubled over and vomited on the street.

I ran all the way back to the Emmonds' house. Keghani sat with Yester at the kitchen table. They both looked frightened. "This is the end of us," she said.

"What if you dressed as Alevis?" I asked. "Please, Keghani," I said. "Take off your crucifix. I'll give you my red silk to braid into your hair. Yester, Aunt Besee could lend you some clothes."

Keghani sadly shook her head. "They have their list of names. If we don't show up for deportation, they'll kill all of you and burn this house down in retribution."

There had to be a way to save them.

June 27, 1915

Dear Ali,

The world has turned all upside down, yet here I sit in Mr. Davis' quiet library, completely safe. It is cool in here, and I am surrounded by books and the faint scent of lemon oil and beeswax. A maid has brought in a tall glass of iced tea and I love the tart sweet taste of it. If I were a different person, I would just stay in this library and never go out. Maybe I could forget about the horrors outside. But I cannot do that. I must help in any way I can. Mr. Davis says that one way I can help is to write about it in these letters to you. He said it's good that I write in Zaza because then if the letters are confiscated, it would take them longer to translate them. There are bad people in every race, of course, but I am fairly certain that the Alevis are against what this government is doing. They would have a hard time finding a Zaza speaker who would betray my words, I think.

The paper that Mr. Davis has given me to write on is thick and creamy. I am not saying that I like this paper better than the journal you gave me. That was given with love, but this writing paper has a feel of authority—like only the truth can be written on it. The consul always leaves out a selection of pens for me, but the one I like best is a black enamel fountain pen filled with bright blue ink. I can write for much longer, as there is no need to keep on dipping the quill into an inkpot. This morning, as I walked the three miles to Mezreh with my shopping bags, my mind churned thinking of the hellish world that surrounds me. People who had lived in this area for thousands of years were being rounded up and killed? I tried to set my emotions aside to make sense of it from the government's point of view. What was their purpose? Did they want all the businesses to grind to a halt and all the shops to all close? What about the hospitals? Without the Armenians, who would run them? Killing the Armenians would even harm the Turks, so why were they doing this?

When the Young Turks came to power, I was jubilant because they had promised equality for all. What I didn't realize back then was that their way to equality was to kill the people they considered non-Turks. They are no better than the sultans. We Alevis have been harassed for centuries for our religious beliefs as well. Mama said that's why the Armenians and Alevis have always been so close; that thousands of years ago, we were one people: "The difference between the Armenians and us is thinner than the skin of an onion." But we have different ways of surviving, don't we, Ali? Armenians had the Christian missionaries to protect them, but we Alevis protect ourselves by blending in. Allah, the Arabic word for God, is the same as Jesus, the sun, the moon, the stars. God is inside of us all. I can outwardly pray to whichever word for God my oppressors want me to—that is not denying God, but simply recognizing him in all of his manifestations. If asked, I could say that I was Muslim and not be lying because I am Muslim—and Jewish and Christian and Shaman. This is our strength over the Armenians.

It is my duty to use my strength, Ali, to save Keghani and Yester and any other Christian that I can.

This morning on my way here, I went to the bazaar and methodically purchased the items I knew that the consul would want: oranges, grapes, freshly baked flat bread, a butchered lamb, fresh vegetables, and olives. As expected, the conversation all around me was about the impending deportation. It filled me with anxiety to listen to people talk about it as calmly as they might discuss the weather. I finished my shopping and repacked the items in my bags to distribute the weight evenly, and began my walk to the Consulate.

I was still a block away when I heard the chanting: "Praise be to Allah. Bless us in our efforts to kill the Christians." I kept on walking, safe in the knowledge that my peasant clothing helped me blend into the crowd.

Across the street from the Consulate building, a huge group of Turks stood and chanted those horrible words: "*Praise be to Allah. Bless us in our efforts to kill the Christians.*" Among them were Muslim Kurds. Even though they were not Alevi, they were still Kurds who had been subjected to government actions themselves in the past, so why were they now siding with the government?

Dozens of Armenians crowded around the Consulate entrance, some waving papers and shouting that they had American citizenship, others weeping. Garabed, Consul Davis' Armenian bodyguard, let them in a few at a time. He saw me at the back of the crowd and caught my eye.

"Zeynep." He whisked me inside. "Go into the library," he said. "There are papers and pens set out for you."

I wrote down the things that happened since last Wednesday, trying to remember all the details. I really needed to talk to the consul, to see what could be done for Keghani and Yester. But when I was finished writing, there were still people in line waiting to see the consul.

I will stay here all night if I have to.

Ali, we have been apart for so long that sometimes I fear I'll forget what you look like. Or maybe your looks have changed drastically like mine have? If you saw me now with this short, stubbly hair and my skin pocked with typhus scabs, would you recognize me? Perhaps you'd turn away in disgust and put me out of your mind.

Dare I admit that I've gone hours without thinking of you at all? It's not that I don't love you—I do—passionately. But there is so much sadness here that I feel it's a betrayal of my friends to have happy memories. I am hoping that when this war is over, I'll be able to get to you. I need to find out for sure if you do still love me, even after all I've been through.

I've been saving the coins the consul has been paying me, hoping that when the war is over I'll be able to buy my own passage to Canada. I know that you said you were saving money too, but it would make me so proud to be able to do this on my own. Wouldn't you be surprised if I knocked on your door in Brantford?

Leslie Davis is an important man in America. I know you're in Canada, but Mr. Davis probably knows Canadian government people too. Maybe he will help me get to you. This is what I hope and pray for. In the meantime, I am trying not to think of you. I must concentrate on my friends who are in danger.

I finally got a chance to talk to the consul. He asked if either Yester or Keghani have family in America. He says that if either is married to an American, he might be able to help them. Keghani is not married, I know that for certain. Yester is married to Onnig, who is not an American. I am devastated by this news. There has to be another way to help them.

July 12, 1915

Dear Ali,

At the end of June, army officials went from house to house marking the doors of people who were to be deported. The Emmonds' house had one mark—for Keghani. Yester's house in the city got two marks, even though Onnig has been gone for some time. Any Armenian found in one of these marked houses after the deportation date was to be shot. Anyone hiding an Armenian was to be shot.

Armenian men still held in the Red Konak were released to assist their families in dissolving their household goods. I had hoped that Toven or Onnig would return, but they didn't. I fear that they're already dead, but pray that they are far away from this area.

No Armenian is allowed to travel with more than twenty lira and all Armenians are to dispose of their worldly goods before they leave. What they cannot sell, they must leave behind. You can imagine the frenzy of selling that has been taking place.

Keghani and I went into the city to help Yester get everything out of her house and onto the street, so she could sell it. We rolled up beautiful carpets, then dragged out antique wooden tables, china plates, silverware, mementos—it all had to go. As I carried out an armload of Yester's precious leather-bound books, a woman, covered from head to toe in black, paused in front of Yester's prized Singer sewing machine.

"That sewing machine doesn't look bad," the woman remarked.

"It's new," said Yester.

"I'll give you this for it," said the woman, holding out her hand. A few coins—enough for a single loaf of bread.

Yester blinked back tears. "It's worth far more than that."

"Take it or leave it."

Yester took it.

The woman grabbed the sewing machine in both arms and walked away.

Turks poured in from all over the countryside, in a festive

mood, happy to snap up the bargains: it was like a holiday to them.

Reverend Emmonds went to the vali and asked him if some of the missionaries could accompany the Armenians on the deportation. The vali refused. It was nearly impossible to find donkeys or oxen to buy or rent, but the vali promised he would provide donkeys himself; that made us all feel a little bit less frightened. Maybe this really was just a deportation, not a death march.

But then, on the day before Keghani and Yester were to leave, several dozen near-dead women and children entered the city on foot. There were no men with them and no boys over the age of ten. Traveling with them was the Hamidiye Alaylari, the cavalry that includes Muslim Kurds, who had been released from prison to help deport Armenians. The men wore army uniforms, and they were fierce. It made me sick to think of any Kurds, even if they weren't Alevi Kurds, doing the government's dirty work. They spoke Turkish, not Zaza, and they seemed almost to enjoy their nasty job.

The group camped out in a public area not far from our house, so I dressed in my Kurdish clothing and bought bread at the market, and I went to speak to them. I noticed another woman mingling with them as well, handing out food. I approached a young mother who was dressed in nothing more than a flimsy rag that barely covered anything. On her lap was a listless baby with hollow cheeks and gray-tinged skin. I ripped off a good portion of bread and handed it to her.

She pushed it away. "I cannot afford it."

I looked at the other woman and realized she was charging

for the food. Did that other woman not feel God inside of her? How could she live with herself, acting so cruelly to people in need?

"I'm not selling this," I said. "I'm giving it to you."

The woman's eyes filled with tears. She took the bread and broke off a bit and put it into her mouth. She chewed it carefully, then opened her baby's mouth and dropped in the masticated bread. Only after the baby had swallowed down several mouthfuls did the woman take any for herself. It was such a tender and caring sight that I was overwhelmed with emotion.

"Where are you from?" I asked.

"Erzurum," she said. "We left on June 7."

They had been marching for nearly a month. Armenians were being marched into Erzurum as well. If this were really a deportation, why were people being marched in circles?

"How many of you were on this march?"

"Hundreds," she said. "We were barely out of the city when we were attacked by Kurds. They killed the men and boys, and stripped us of our clothing."

"Not all Kurds are working with the government," I told her. "I'm an Alevi Kurd myself."

"Thank God for people like you," she said. "There were Alevi Kurds who came down from the mountain and secretly gave us clothing and some food when they could. But we were marched again. Each day, more people died, some of thirst or disease; others were killed. We are all that's left."

I gave her another piece of bread, then stepped through

those sorry people and handed out everything else that I had.

Early the next morning I went back, but the woman and her baby were gone. The group had dwindled to half the size of yesterday. I asked another woman where she went. "The baby died," she said. "The mother was killed."

"And the others?"

"Most died, but a couple of the girls were taken."

Her words filled me with despair. I handed out the rest of my bread in silence, hoping it would bring a measure of comfort to these poor unfortunates whose existence could be measured in hours.

As I walked back to the Emmonds' house, I was filled with foreboding. This was the day that Keghani and Yester were to be deported. I visualized them a few weeks from now, starving and ragged in some unknown place—if they were still alive. I could not let that fate happen to them. Yester had gone to her own house, waiting for the soldiers to come for her. I had no idea how to help her, but when I returned to the Emmonds', I found Keghani sitting at the kitchen table, a knapsack beside her packed with dried bread and a large jug of water with a rope around the neck sitting on the floor beside her. The vali's promised donkeys were nowhere in sight and this was all she could carry. How long would it last out in the desert?

"You must wear my clothing," I said. "That way, the soldiers will think you're a Kurd."

Keghani's eyebrows rose. "I don't see how that will help."

"Don't argue." I took off my long embroidered tunic and

draped it across the back of one of the kitchen chairs. Then I untied my sash and handed it to her. I slipped my thin cotton dress over my head. As I stood there in nothing but my gauzy under-tunic and trousers, I wondered if my plan would work.

"Hurry," I said. "Take off your clothing and put these on."

Keghani stood up and unbuttoned her western-style blouse. She slipped off her skirt. "Your crucifix too," I said.

Her hands flew up to her neck. "I can't take this off."

"No arguments."

Sighing deeply, Keghani undid the chain. She held the crucifix in her hand for a moment, then brushed it with her lips. "This was my grandmother's," she said.

"I'll keep it safe."

I ran upstairs. Aunt Besee wasn't there—she'd spent the night at Yester's house. Fatma was sitting cross-legged on the floor, playing a game with Suleyman. I told her of my plan for Keghani and what I still needed. Fatma rooted through the wardrobe that she and I shared with Aunt Besee. "This would be a good scarf for her," she said, giving me a silky red one.

"Thank you, cousin." I was nearly out the door when Fatma called me back.

"Keghani should wear this as well," she said, unfastening the chain from around her neck—it was her own evil eye.

"Are you sure?" I asked, touched that she would part with the good luck stone she'd worn since she was a baby.

"I am sure. Anything to help Keghani."

When I got back downstairs I wrapped the red scarf around Keghani's hair, and looped the chain around her neck. She picked up the glittering green stone between her two fingers. "The evil eye?" she said. "This is blasphemous."

"Keghani," I said with more than a little bit of frustration. "It's not blasphemous. It's for good luck. And it makes you look less Christian."

She walked over to the mirror in the hallway and gazed at herself. She turned to face me then, and her eyes were filled with gratitude. "I still don't know what you're up to, but I thank you for trying."

I scooted her out the door, shoving a few coins in her hand. "Pretend you're me," I said. "Go down to the Mezreh market and buy fresh fruit, vegetables, bread. Take it to the American Consulate and ask for Garabed. Recite for him the fourth verse of Psalm 23, so he'll know I sent you. Do not leave the Consulate grounds once you're inside. You'll be safe as long as you stay there."

Now that Keghani was safely out of the house, one problem remained. The soldiers would insist on taking someone.

Still wearing nothing but my undergarments, I gathered Keghani's clothing and took them upstairs.

"Is Keghani out of the house now?" asked Fatma.

"Yes," I said. "Pray that she stays safe."

Fatma took the clothing from my arms and laid each item out on the bed. "I have an idea of what you're planning and I think you're crazy." She gave me a sideways glance. "You're going to pretend to be Keghani, so they won't go looking for her."

"That's right," I said. "The trick will be finding the right opportunity to reveal that I'm not Armenian once we're well out of the city."

"It will be risky, but you always have been daring, and I admire you for that," said Fatma.

I was overwhelmed by her remarks. You know that I have always been a little bit different, Ali, and I hope that's why you love me, but it has gotten me into trouble countless times. Knowing that Fatma accepted me felt like a balm to my soul.

Keghani's crucifix slipped out of the clothing and fell to the floor. Fatma picked it up. "Turn around, so I can fasten this around your neck."

I did as she said, trying to hide my tears.

Fatma stepped over to the wardrobe and took out a pale mauve dress that Yester had sewn for her. "This will be better than yours," she said. "It's thin enough to wear under your American clothing and pale enough that the color won't show through."

I slipped it over my head, and tied a red satiny belt around my waist. I put my plain white blouse over top and buttoned it to my neck, then slipped the gold chain out over the collar so the crucifix dangled prominently just below my chin. I stepped into my long dark gray skirt and buttoned it up, then buckled on the leather belt. Despite wearing two outfits in the middle of the summer, I shivered with apprehension.

Fatma folded up my older embroidered tunic, tied it with a bright blue headscarf, and carried the bundle downstairs. I followed. She put the bundled tunic into the bread-filled knapsack. I stepped in front of the mirror as Fatma stood behind me. Her eyes reflected her worry, but her mouth was held in a small smile. She was petrified with fear about what I was about to do, but trusted me to know my mind. My reflection surprised me: the fierce determination in my heart did not show on my face. I looked like an average girl. My hair had grown in a couple of inches and was now a mass of messy black curls. My face had lost the sick sallow complexion. My eyes were immediately drawn to the gold cross under my chin, which was good. Anyone who looked at me would see that first. No one would think I was anything other than Armenian. Besides, what was the physical difference between an Armenian and an Alevi Kurdish girl?

I sat at the kitchen table to wait for the soldiers. Suleyman scrambled onto my lap and I wrapped my arms around him, nuzzling my face into his hair. As I held him, I thought of you, Ali. What would you think if you knew what I was up to? Would you be proud of me or angry that I was taking such risks? If you were in my position, you would do the same thing. We are separated by half a world, dear Ali, but you are my other half.

Lenore and the reverend came home before the time the soldiers arrived. When Lenore saw me packed and waiting, wearing Keghani's crucifix, she gasped. "Where is Keghani?"

"Safe," I said.

"You cannot go in her place," said Lenore. "You'll be walking to certain death."

"Someone has to go," I said. "So please go along with this. Otherwise you are all in danger."

Suddenly we heard shouts and banging outside. The soldiers had arrived on our street. Rather than be passive about it, I met my fate head-on. I kissed Suleyman's head one last time and stood up. Pulling on the knapsack, I grasped the earthen water jug and stepped out onto the street with the doomed Armenians.

Oh, my dear Ali,

It was so terrifying to be marched out of town with thousands of others as the hot sun beat down on us. My jug of water nearly slipped and shattered within two blocks of the Emmonds' house and sweat trickled down my brow and from my armpits. How could any of us make it all the way to Urfa like this?

Usually I can walk down to Mezreh in less than an hour, but with so many babies and toddlers and old people, and so many items to carry, the crowd moved slowly. We weren't past Mezreh until late afternoon. The mounted Hamidiye Alaylari surrounded us. I searched through the crowds, looking for Yester. She was close to the rear of the column. As I stepped in beside her, her face was something to behold.

"Where's Keghani?" she whispered.

"Safe. I'll try to save you too. Stay with me."

Yester nodded. We marched in silence for another hour or so.

When the sun began to set, the soldiers got off their horses and directed us to settle in for the night at the side of the road. Mothers passed out dried pieces of bread and cups of water for their children. Once the meager meal was finished, they curled up with their children. Within an hour, most everyone was asleep.

Under the moonlight, I lay down too and closed one eye. Yester was wide awake beside me. I quietly slipped off my American clothing and draped it over top of myself until I was able to pull the embroidered tunic out of my knapsack and put it on. Then I gave the bright blue scarf to Yester who solemnly covered her hair with it. When she was finished she pointed to the crucifix around my neck. I unclasped it and was going to put it into my knapsack, but Yester held out her hand. I gave it to her and she slipped it into her pocket, then removed her own.

I heard faint rustling sounds around me and squinted my eyes to make out the shapes in the moonlight. The glitter of a knife. Silhouettes of Hamidiye Alaylari skulking through the deportees. I saw one pick up a child and carry her away. Then I heard the wet snick of a knife through flesh.

And again.

Suddenly, a uniformed Kurd towered above me, curved blade held high.

I sat up, letting my American clothing fall to the side and my Kurdish outfit show. "Allah is great," I whispered in Turkish.

The blade faltered. I jumped up and grabbed Yester's hand. We ran.

Away from the road, into the woods, up, up, up a rocky incline. Footsteps thumping behind us. Yester tripped. We couldn't go much farther. Wordlessly, I directed Yester to hide behind a rock.

I stood in the middle of the pathway, hands on hips. A different uniformed Kurd approached, breathless. "Which way did the Armenians go?" he asked in Turkish.

I pointed. He ran. Then I grabbed Yester's hand again and we went in the opposite direction.

We walked up as high as we could, huffing from anxiety as much as from exhaustion. Suddenly there was a clearing—a small village. I walked up to the first house and tapped on the door, calling out in Zaza, "Please help us!"

An old woman opened the door and her eyes widened when she saw me. "You're an Alevi Kurd?" she asked.

"Yes, from Eyolmez," I said.

"Why were you being deported?"

"A long story," I said. "Can my mother and I hide here?"

She looked dubiously over at Yester. I don't think she believed she was my mother. The woman sighed. "You don't have to lie to me," she said. "I will help you."

Ali, she took us into her house that night. Soldiers banged at her door. She threw blankets over to cover us, before she opened up. They stood there, knives and clothing slick with blood and I was afraid that this was the end of us.

"Have you seen any Armenians," they asked her in Turkish.

"No," she said.

They didn't leave right away, but instead came in and washed their clothing and their knives. The woman gave them something to eat and they left.

I stayed awake all night, waiting for more knocks at the door.

"I'll take you to another village farther up the mountain," said the old woman early the next morning. "You'll be safer there."

As we walked, we talked. "The Hamidiye Alaylari do the devil's work just so they could be released from jail," she said. "And they think that because we are also Kurds that we agree with what they do. But once all the Armenians are killed, the Turks will come after the Kurds. The minorities must stick together or we're all dead."

The village was very high up in the Dersim Mountains, overlooking the Euphrates River. The people spoke Zaza with a sprinkling of Armenian just like in Eyolmez. I recognized a man who had been to our hospital with a foot injury. He greeted me with a broad grin and showed me how well his foot was healing.

"We were never introduced formally," he said. "My name is Gernaz. You and your Armenian friend are safe here as long as you want to stay."

We stayed there for three days—long enough for the deportees' caravan to move—and Yester is still up there now, safe and hiding.

October 1, 1915

Dear Ali,

Here I am again, sitting in the library at the American Consulate. I am so filled with despair that I can barely lift this pen to write, but Consul Davis tells me that I must.

I am an eyewitness.

Most of the eyewitnesses are missionaries or Armenian survivors and Mr. Davis feels that it is important to have a local who isn't Christian to document the events as well—but where to start?

First, I am so very grateful that you are not here. This place is hell on earth.

I wish I could know what you are doing, although I find great comfort in imagining that you are living in safety. Consul Davis has shown me photographs of America and everything looks so clean and new. Do they have tall buildings in Brantford and do all of the ladies wear hats? Are there wide streets and motor cars and lots of food?

I have been unable to write because I am so utterly busy. I work as many hours as I can at the hospital. In addition to injured soldiers from the front, we have Armenians who have escaped the deportations and made their way back here. It is not safe for them to stay at the hospital, so we treat them quickly, and they hide in abandoned houses, in cemeteries, under doorsteps—wherever they can. Since many of the doctors and nurses have been deported, the few who are left here must work through their exhaustion. I do whatever I can to help.

Three days after I escaped the deportation with Yester, I left her in the mountain village and walked back to Harput. On my way, I encountered many decaying corpses of deportees who had been stripped naked and left on the roadside. Many died clutching babies. What a terrible world this is, when human beings are treated like garbage.

I knocked on the Emmonds' door a week to the day from when I left. Aunt Besee opened the door and pulled me inside. Her eyes were filled with tears of joy. Suleyman shrieked and clutched my knees. "Don't go away ever again, Aunt Zeynep," he said. I was dusty and hungry and tired, but I picked him up and hugged him tight, burying my nose in his hair. All at once, my strength left. I wept. It was so good to be safe and surrounded by people I loved, but how could I be happy when I had witnessed a trail of tragedy all along the road?

"Where is Fatma?" I asked.

"Working in the hospital, buying food in the market for the consul," said Aunt Besee. "She didn't want to leave Sulyeman, but after you left, she decided she had to put other people's needs before her own."

"And Keghani?"

"She is safe at the Consulate. What about Yester?"

"In the Dersim Mountains, hiding in a friendly Alevi Kurdish village."

Gernaz, my Dersim friend, has come back to the hospital more than once with news. "Yester gives you her blessing," he said.

"She's looking after some of the children who have escaped. We'll keep them safe even if we have to fight the soldiers to the death."

"May God bless you for your good work, Gernaz," I said, taking his hand in mine.

"We cannot stand by and see innocent people killed."

"I wish the Kurds who become Hamidiye Alaylari felt the same way," I said. "They give all Kurds a bad name."

"Those Kurds are not from around here and they do not share our religion," said Gernaz. "They don't have Armenians as their neighbors like we do. Our fate is almost as precarious as the Armenians. We live in the mountains with Turkey on one side and Russia on the other. And we'll defend our mountains to the death."

A few weeks ago, an Alevi Kurd whom I didn't know came to the hospital asking for me. I stepped outside to meet with him. "I have seventeen Armenian children with me," he said. "Can you take them?"

"Where are they now?"

"Just outside the city gates," he said. "I cannot get them past the guards. We hid them in our village for several weeks, but it's getting too dangerous to keep them."

I found Reverend Emmonds and told him about the children. I have no idea how he managed it, but he brought the orphans into the city and they're now safe in the American orphanage.

Practically every day all summer, caravans of exhausted and

threadbare Armenians marched past Harput. They are not from around here. Consul Davis learned that they had been brought in by train from the farthest reaches of the country. And why? To be marched in circles in the desert until they die. Because we are in the middle of nowhere out here, the government thinks that nobody sees what they do.

Leslie Davis has taken photographs and he has tried to send telegrams out to let the world know what's going on and to ask for help, but they never reach their destination. The missionaries' telephones have been confiscated, letters censored, and photographs destroyed. Meanwhile Armenians continue to die. Mr. Davis estimates that a million and a half Armenians have been killed. Is that even possible? Each of those million and a half people was a living, breathing human being like you or me.

Inside the Consulate, in this very library where I sit and write, Consul Davis has a large and secure safe. Inside it he keeps many important papers, including my journal and my letters. But he also stores precious identity papers for Armenians who have some claim to American citizenship. He also keeps the deportees' money safely locked up.

Some survivors trickle back, mostly old women and very young boys, but where can they live? The houses that were owned by wealthy Armenians have been taken over by army officers and are guarded by soldiers. The poorer homes were destroyed: wood and roofs pulled off, windows shattered. Some people sleep in these ruined houses, but when winter sets in, what then?

Consul Davis is hiding many refugees right here in the Consulate building. Keghani is here, but I don't see her very often. Like all of the Armenians, she knows how to hide. At this very moment, there are eighty people, including some men. At night, they all sleep outside under the mulberry trees. During the day, the women quietly keep to the shadows outside. The tall wall protects them from prying eyes, but someone could scale the wall, couldn't they? The few men who are here dare not step outside during the day. They stay in the attic. All through this hot summer, they remained in the attic, still as mice.

The consul does his best to wrangle papers out of the government. If a refugee has an American relative, it is often possible to get them out of the country. As soon as a person is given safe passage out, another one comes to the consul to take their place. It is a never-ending job. There are far too many dead to keep track of—just think of that, Ali. But Consul Davis does what he can. When he hears of the death of someone with American ties, he sets their identity papers aside. He doesn't destroy them but saves them. I think he may be using them to save the survivors. Of course he pretends that this is not the case.

Aunt Besee, Fatma, and Suleyman are now here with me. They go to the market and buy food, and they help to prepare it as well. The consul has kitchen staff, but he's sure that some are spies, so it's safer when we look after the refugees' food.

Consul Davis entertains army and government officials, holding banquets and playing cards. The vali himself is here nearly every day and considers the consul a great friend. Are his guests truly unaware of what he's doing, or will they descend upon these helpless people at an unexpected time and kill them? I need to get Keghani out of here, but how? I have to wait until the time is right.

In the midst of all this death, I've seen much goodness. Many Turks are appalled at their government's action. "It is not Allah's will that we kill our neighbors," said one man who carried in his arms an emaciated woman who had collapsed on his doorstep. "The wrath of Allah will come down upon us all for what the government claims we've been doing in His name."

The director of the Red Crescent hospital is also a kind man. He has taken in nearly a thousand Armenians, and because he is an important Muslim, the vali turns a blind eye. Women, fully draped in chadors, go to the caravans and hand out bread.

And there are many Armenians who, like Yester, have hidden in the Dersim Mountains, but in all of these situations, the Armenians are only safe for now. How will they get out of Turkey?

November 4, 1915

Dear Ali,

It is getting colder as each day passes and the Armenians can no longer sleep outside. The Consulate building is huge, but there are now nearly 100 refugees here. It is a precarious situation. During the day and into the evening, Leslie Davis must entertain government and army officials, and appear friendly. The attics are crammed with people all day, then at night, they come down and sleep on the floor in the huge entrance.

Fatma, Suleyman, Aunt Besee, and I are not sleeping here since it has turned cold and is so crowded inside. The Emmonds have hidden Armenians at their house, so we cannot go there either. Aunt Besee found us shelter in one of the small abandoned homes in the Armenian district that is of no interest to the officers. The windows are all broken and it smelled like an outhouse, but she cleaned it up and now it is our temporary home.

When I stand on the rooftop, I see snow on the mountains in the distance and it reminds me of home. How I wish I could turn back time to when there was no war and no deportations, to when you were by my side.

Stay safe, dear Ali, and think of me now and again.

November 20, 1915

Dear Ali,

Armenians who have taken shelter on this side of the Dersim Mountains are stranded there for now, but they are treated well by the Alevi Kurds so they can bide their time. I've heard that some adventurous souls have trekked to the Russian side of the mountain, and from there to freedom. Most are waiting for the advance of the Russian Army—then the trickle will turn into a flow.

But it's not the people who are already in the Dersim Mountains that we're concerned about—it's the Armenians still in Harput, especially the few men who are still alive. How do they get to the mountains? They must first leave the city without being caught, then cross the Euphrates River, which is blocked by soldiers from Constantinople.

November 21, 1915

Gurnaz has found a guard at the Euphrates who will take a bribe and has asked Leslie Davis for the money.

November 22, 1915

Dear Ali,

Keghani escaped with two Armenian men. They covered themselves from head to foot in chadors, and a sympathetic Turkish man walked them through the city gates and stayed with them until they were out on the open road. Gurnaz met them after dark at an appointed spot, and they continued their journey to the Euphrates, where they crossed safely. The bribe worked.

The Alevi Kurds on the other side guided them into the mountains. Keghani and her companions are hiding in a village close to the Russian border. We've only saved three people so far, but this is the most hopeful news I have had in a very long time.

December 31, 1915

Dear Ali,

The year has ended on a devastating note. When I was working in the hospital today, a soldier who had lost one eye called me to his bed. "I heard you're from Eyolmez," he said. "I didn't think anyone survived from there."

My heart sunk. "I left before the war. What do you know about Eyolmez?"

"I was sent there in the summer to round up the Armenians. They're all dead." He tilted his head and looked at my face, "But you're not Armenian, are you?"

"No, I am an Alevi. The last I heard, my mother was hiding in the mountains."

"With the Armenians?"

"She would have been hiding with her neighbors."

"She's gone too, then," he said. "We cleared the whole area."

There is nothing left for me in this cursed country. I intend to leave, even if I die in the process. I want Aunt Besee and Fatma out, and especially Suleyman. I do not want my nephew growing up here. He must know freedom. He must meet his father.

We could get through to the Dersim. The soldiers wouldn't stop us of course. Even the Hamidiye Alaylari don't realize that not all Kurds are Muslim and not all Kurds are working with the government. For us, it would be possible to travel to the mountains and stay there where it's safer.

The trick would be to escape to the West from there. Also, there is much work to do before we leave. Many Armenians need our help.

January 2, 1916

Dear Ali,

The consul says that we cannot go to Canada because it is at war with Turkey. Although America is not at war with Turkey, the only people he can get out are the ones who have relatives in America.

Have you been put in the Canadian army, Ali? If so, I hope you have a uniform and food. I am beyond despair. The thought of you safe in Canada had been my one shred of hope. If you have died, all I have left is to make sure that Suleyman grows up in freedom.

Aunt Besee is a forgotten wife. I don't even remember Uncle Adir. He hasn't visited or written in years, but she says he is in Detroit in America. Consul Davis says that may mean he has become an American citizen, so he is looking into it. It may turn out to be a blessing that her husband abandoned her all those years ago if it means she can get out now.

And me? I have no claims at all.

January 10, 1916

Gurnaz came to the Consulate from the mountains today dressed in many layers against the cold. He took off his cap and pulled out a stained and worn square of paper. A letter for the consul, but he let me read it first:

Dear Consul Davis,

Thank the Lord that I am now safe in Russia. Without your assistance, I would never have made it. I had entrusted you with my papers and 112 dollars cash, and I ask that you give these now to Gurnaz, who will get them to me. If my wife and daughter are still under your protection, I ask that you allow them to leave with Gurnaz when he feels that it is safe.

With thanks and praise,
Taniel Aloian

As I read, Gurnaz removed his winter boot and dug through the lining until he retrieved a second letter:

Dear Leslie Davis,

My sister and I are now on the other side of the Dersim under the Russian Army's protection. Just as the black slaves had brave souls running the Underground Railroad to freedom during the American Civil War, we have the Alevi Kurds to lead us to freedom through the Dersim Mountains. I have 100 dollars kept in your safe. I do not want this for myself. Please give it to Gurnaz so he can get more Armenians out.

Yours sincerely,
Molly Zakarian

Gurnaz removed his other boot, and gave me this note with a smile:

Dear Zeynep,
I am safe with the Russians. If not for you, I would not be alive.
Thank you, sister of my heart, for all that you have done.
Love,
Keghani

January 14, 1916

Dear Ali,

It comforts me to stand on the snowy roof of this shattered house in the destroyed Armenian section of Mezreh and look out to the mountains. Their stark white beauty takes my breath away. I think of all my dead loved ones scattered on our own mountains above Eyolmez. They are at peace now, I know that, but I miss them so much.

When I close my eyes, I imagine you standing here beside me. I think of you draping your coat over my cold shoulders and promising to always keep me safe, but when I open my eyes you are gone.

I have no one to rely on except myself.

January 22, 1916

The Russian Army made a surprise attack on the Ottoman Army at Koprukoy. They've pushed the Turks all the way back to the fortress at Erzurum. This is the chance we've been waiting for. We are getting as many Armenians through to the Dersim as we possibly can. Thousands may go over the mountains to Russia.

March 21, 1916

Oh, dear Ali,

I fear these may be the last words I ever write. The Turks of Harput and Mezreh are preparing to flee. The Dersim Alevi Kurds have joined with the Russians and are approaching the city. I am in the middle of this and have no way of getting out.

The Ottoman Army, assisted by Muslim Kurds, are fighting back. Aunt Besee, Fatma, Suleyman, and I fled to the American Consulate for protection. Leslie Davis says that the vali will deport all of the Alevis just like they deported the Armenians. The vali wants to kill every one of us. Why didn't I go to the Dersim when there was still time? Ali, will you ever forgive me? And will Yousef forgive me if Suleyman dies?

March 25, 1916

We are hiding quietly in the attic of the Consulate building. I don't know what will happen to Leslie Davis if the vali discovers that he is hiding Alevis. When I part the curtain, I glimpse the street beyond the walls that protect the Consulate grounds. Thousands of Alevi Kurds—men, women, children, babies— marching out the city gates. Will they all be massacred like the Armenians? Who will save us?

A strange sound in the streets. More crying, wailing, shouts. Have they rounded up yet more Alevi Kurds?

When will this stop?

PART SIX

KAPUSKASING, ONTARIO

March 1915

The thought of someone coming into Prison Island while I was
away sent a shiver through me. McPhee or Donaldson would
report me in an instant. I was doomed.

How could I have been so stupid? If it was on my record
that I had tried to escape, would I be able to get my citizenship?
How would I get Zeynep to Canada?

I paced the small cabin, willing time to speed up. Someone,
please come and tell me my fate! I pummeled the cabin door
with my fists, making a bloody mess of them both. Maybe I
should have gone north with Nadie after all. At least then I
would have some sort of life.

I collapsed on the cot and somehow slept.

Was it hours, or days when the door finally opened? I had lost all track of time. But it wasn't McPhee and it wasn't Donaldson. Officer Wilkin himself stepped in.

I scrambled to my feet and stood at attention.

"My God, man. What did you do to your hands?"

I held them behind my back. "It's nothing, sir, just a few small cuts."

"The important thing is that you've come back," said Wilkin. "I thought you'd run off for good."

I held my breath.

"At ease, Ali."

I exhaled.

"I haven't reported you. And perhaps I won't. But I need you to tell me how you managed to get out of Prison Island."

The whole story spilled out, about Tomas being rude to Nadie in the church and in the store, about her coming here and taking me away.

"And yet you came back."

"My dream is to become a Canadian, to bring my betrothed to Canada. Leaving with Nadie was tempting," I said. "But I just couldn't do it."

"It's good that you can think into the future," Wilkin said. "Not many of the prisoners here can do that. Not many of the enlisted men either, for that matter."

"Thank you, sir."

He looked down at my shredded knuckles. "Next time you

want to take out your anger, think into the future. Do you really want to be cutting down trees with hands like that?"

"No, sir."

He nodded. "I'm glad you came back. Please do not tell any of the other prisoners about your escape. This is our secret."

We rowed back to the main camp that same day, and when I walked into Bunkhouse 5, it felt like coming home. Yousef had stockpiled his rations of vegetables and potatoes for me and cooked them into a hearty stew. That night, I played cards with my some of my bunkmates and reveled in the company of friends. This place was a prison camp, but it was also my refuge.

The next morning, as we stood at attention for roll call, Officer Wilkin asked the inmates of Bunkhouse 5 to remain. "I have a new job for you," he said. "Follow me."

He led all of us Alevis to a clearing close to the banks of the Kapuskasing River. "We have a lady schoolteacher coming," he said, "to teach the children of the soldiers here. And that schoolteacher is engaged to Private McPhee."

He swept his arms at the clearing in front of us. "They'll need a place to live, so I want you to build them a log cabin right here."

"Do you want it to be the same layout as the bunkhouses?" Yousef asked.

Officer Wilkin regarded my brother. "You built houses in Brantford before the war, didn't you?"

Yousef nodded.

"Did you make anything nicer than the bunkhouses?"

"We did, sir," he said. "But we used bricks. I'll do the best that I can with wood."

"Draw up the blueprints," Wilkin said. "I don't promise that I'll be able to get everything needed to make this like a house in the south, but we'll do our best."

Yousef grinned broadly. "Yes, sir."

September 1915

The new assignment made the spring and summer go by quickly and I was impressed with the small touches that Yousef added to the basic bunkhouse design to make it into an attractive and comfortable home: a sanded and sealed wooden floor, plaster on the walls, more windows, a verandah and front steps.

It was good to work outside on something different and not to be in the woods. At lunchtime, I'd sit on a large stump, watch the dark swirling river, and wonder what my life would have been if I hadn't returned to the camp. Mostly I thought of Zeynep and wondered how the war was affecting her. With Russia so close, I knew she could be living near the warzone. How I wish I could speak to her or see her to make sure she was safe. I thought of Nadie too. Had the whites let her into one of their schools? If not, I was sure she'd figure out a way around it. She was that kind of person.

Emily the schoolteacher came at the end of July and the camp administration was in a frenzy to greet her and hold a full military wedding for her and McPhee. The officer's mess even baked an impressive three-tiered wedding cake.

The prisoners were naturally not invited, but we had the halfday off and we could watch the festivities from a distance. I was happy for the couple, but I was jealous too. Emily was safe. She was here.

For all I knew, my Zeynep was dead.

A light dusting of snow fell overnight on the last Sunday in September and it made me realize that soon we'd be plunged into winter yet again. During free time after roll call, I walked around the parade grounds, deep in thought. This place had changed dramatically since I arrived ten months ago, when the few bunkhouses were nearly enveloped in trees. Now the prison was huge, with row upon row of bunkhouses, and a vast strip of land denuded of forest. The ground had thawed sufficiently over the summer that two layers of barbed-wire fencing had gone up, separating the prisoners' quarters from the parts of the camp used by the soldiers. It was a crime to take this beautiful piece of wilderness and turn it into a prison. And what of Nadie and her people? The bigger this prison became, the harder it would be for them to hunt and trap. The government had taken away my freedom and forced me to destroy her way of life.

Even Prison Island had changed in the last months. Instead of a solitary confinement cabin, there was a row of them built by my bunkmates. No special touches on *those* buildings. Each was as mean and crude as the one that imprisoned me in the spring.

New prisoners came by train each and every week. Some came from the Spirit Lake camp in the east and others came from Toronto in the south. Whenever there was trouble at another camp, those inmates were shipped to Kapuskasing.

I was so lost in my thoughts that I didn't notice Bohdan walking beside me until he said hello.

"You'll never guess where I'm going," he said, a wide grin on his face.

"Jasper Internment camp?" I asked. "Or maybe Spirit Lake?"

"No," he said. "Welland. To work on the canal. They're paroling me."

I stopped. "Parole?"

"Yes," he said. "There's a labor shortage. They need factory workers and laborers, what with all the able young men fighting in the war."

"So you get set free?"

Bohdan shook his head. "If only it were that easy," he said. "I'll still be a prisoner. I won't be able to leave the city and will have to report weekly to a parole officer, but I'll be paid my full wages."

"Not just twenty-five cents a day like here?"

"I'll be paid good wages and will be able to send it home to my wife in Alberta. This will be very good for her."

I slapped him on the back, "You deserve this, Bohdan. I wish you well."

"Hope to see you there," he said. "Wouldn't it be great if we were both paroled to the same company?"

I would have loved it if that is what had happened—to earn real money again would mean that I could pay for Zeynep's passage, but it wasn't to be.

"We need you here, Ali," said Wilkin. "Your brother, you, all of Bunkhouse 5. I don't want to break you up. There are still more buildings we need for the camp—better houses for the officers, recreation facilities."

"Will we be paid a regular wage?" I asked.

"No, Ali. You're still at the prison camp. They'll pay us and you'll get your twenty-five cents a day. The rest will go into the government treasury. Think of this as your sacrifice to Canada's war effort."

January 1916

Who would have thought that the war would still be going on after all this time? The weather here is deathly cold. More prisoners have been sent here and the new ones are unruly. Bunkhouses 12 and 13 have gone on strike.

February 1916

I hear so little news about the war. Mostly, all I can do is read the bits of stories from the ripped-up newspapers we're given to stuff our boots with, but the dates are mixed up and the stories torn in half. At night I toss and turn, and worry about what's happening—to Zeynep, to our village, and our country. From the snippets I read, it is not good.

But there was one half-torn newspaper article that gave me hope for Nadie. It wasn't a story about her, but about a different native woman named Charlotte Monture. No nursing school in Canada would take her, so she went to the New Rochelle Hospital School of Nursing in New York and became a nurse two years ago! If Charlotte could do it, so could Nadie.

I had a letter from Hagop. Six Armenians arrived in Brantford from Turkey with alarming news from home. Dear God, can it be true? Has the government marched all of the Armenians of Turkey out into the desert to die? Hagop says few people survived. The ink was smudged with Hagop's tears. He has no word about the Eyolmez Armenians' fate, but I fear the worst. And what of the Alevi Quarter? When the Turks kill Armenians, Alevis are always next in line. I wish there was some way I could get news from her. I pray to God that she is safe.

I cannot live without her.

May 1916

A few days ago, 200 more prisoners were sent to our camp. They came from Petawawa—a ten-hour train ride from the southeast. They were cold and hungry, and more than a few of them looked like they had been maltreated—cut cheeks, bandaged hands, blackened eyes.

They were put in the bunkhouse next to ours. At roll call the next day they were given their assignments, but all of them refused to work.

"We're prisoners of war," shouted a man named Simon, who seemed to be their leader. "We are not your slaves."

His audacity shocked me at first, but I agreed with him. Since December 1914, I have been doing hard labor for virtually no pay. And who benefits? The government. If they keep on getting our labor for nothing, why would they bother closing the camps? Our slave labor fills the government's treasury.

Officer Wilkin stepped in front of Simon. "If you refuse to work, you'll be taken to Prison Island."

Simon shrugged. "You'll have to feed me."

"With bread and water," said Officer Wilkin. "And you'll be in solitary confinement."

Simon said nothing for a moment, but then he turned and looked at the rest of his men. "And what if none of us agree to work?"

"Then you'll all be put on Prison Island."

"So be it," said Simon. He gestured for his mates to follow

him as he walked back to the bunkhouse.

"Halt!" shouted Wilkin.

The men kept walking.

Wilkin raised his gun to the sky and shot. Dozens of camp guards and soldiers arrived within minutes, guns pointed at Simon and his bunkmates.

There is much that I can tolerate, but a bully isn't one of them. I turned to look at Yousef and he nodded. "Let's protect them," I shouted to everyone in hearing distance.

About 300 of us longtime prisoners stepped between Simon's group and the soldiers. I had been in solitary confinement. I knew how awful it was. These men didn't deserve to go there. All they'd done was request that they be treated as prisoners of war and not slaves.

The soldiers didn't back down. Pushing and shoving. More shots rang. Simon was shot.

And so was I.

Late May 1916

The bullet hit me in the thigh. I was carried to the camp hospital on a stretcher and taken to surgery. They dug the bullet out and made me stay in the hospital for a few days. I have to see the medic once a day to have the area cleaned, and I use a crutch, but the doctor says I'll heal up fine, maybe just a limp. In the meantime, I'm peeling potatoes for my bunkmates.

Simon was fortunate. A bullet whizzed by his face, grazing his cheek and taking off a chunk of his ear. Had he turned his head just slightly, the bullet would have pierced his brain.

He's not working and neither are his bunkmates. They're not on Prison Island, but they only are being given bread and water. There are rumblings in the camp that there may be a strike. How I wish I could be paroled like Bohdan has been.

But who would want a laborer on crutches?

PART SEVEN

Chapter One

KARS, RUSSIA

July 17, 1916

Dear Ali,

It has been quite some time since I've been able to put pen to paper, so I will tell you what happened on that fateful day in March. It was a miracle. The 2,000 Alevi Kurds who were about to be massacred were freed. Consul Davis came up to the attic to tell us the news. All the Alevi tribes in the Dersim Mountains had united as one powerful force, threatening to burn the entire city of Harput and everyone in it if the Alevi prisoners were not immediately set free. The Ottoman Army may be strong, but they fear the Dersim Alevi Kurds and they relented. Mr. Davis said that we all had to leave with the armed Dersim Kurds. It was our best chance.

He wordlessly ushered us into the library. On the desk were forged documents. My name was now Zeynep Alevian, I was born in Niagara Falls, Canada, and currently lived at 143 Darling Street in Brantford—your address! Fatma and Suleyman's last name was changed from Hassan to Hassian to make them sound Armenian. He said we would not be questioned so carefully this way, as there are many Armenian women in Canada, but not Alevi Kurdish. Fatma's address is the same as yours and mine. These documents will only work once we're in Russia, because Canada and Russia are allies.

My journal and letters sat neatly beside the documents. "Getting out your written account of what's gone on here is more important than your lives," said Consul Davis. "You need to hide these. You'll be escorted by the Dersim soldiers, but if you're caught by the Turks, these papers cannot be found." He gestured to a length of thin silk on the desktop. "Wrap the documents in this silk and wear them."

"Mr. Davis," I said. "Can you take Suleyman out to the hall-way for a few minutes?" The consul nodded and led the little boy away.

As soon as the door closed, I stripped off my clothes until I was standing there in nothing but my thin tunic and trousers. Fatma ripped the pages out of my journal—the binding was too bulky to hide. She wrapped the pages in the thin silk and bound them tightly to the small of my back. I quickly got dressed. It was Fatma's turn then. She stripped down and we bundled the letters in a second silk packet for her to wear under her clothes.

I tucked away the forged documents and we stepped out of the library. Suleyman ran up to Fatma and she picked him up. We strode to the door.

"Good luck," said Consul Davis, a solemn expression on his face.

"And you," I said. "Many thanks for all you've done."

He nodded slightly, then reached into his pocket. "I almost forgot. This is for you."

He handed me a thick envelope. I nodded my thanks and tucked it into my clothing. It was much later when I realized what it contained—not only cash but an official letter from the American consul to the American Ambassador, David Francis, in Russia, requesting that he facilitate our travel to Canada.

Not all of those 2,000 Alevi Kurd men, women, and children were going on the long walk to the Dersim. Some scattered, returning to their own homes in the villages and hamlets in the area. It was the middle of winter and bitterly cold. There were no donkeys or horses to spare, so everything we needed had to be carried. Leslie Davis found warm coats for us. Fatma and I took turns carrying Suleyman. That first night, we walked for fourteen hours without stopping. Our group was escorted by dozens of fierce Dersim Kurdish soldiers on horseback and the sight of them made me feel protected. Even so, we were in constant danger of ambush and they moved us with urgency.

Suleyman seemed to understand the gravity of the situation. For a six-year-old child, he has seen far too much tragedy. He did not whimper or complain, and Fatma and I took turns carrying him.

We walked up steep hills and down valleys and through icy passes, slipping in frozen streams and gashing our knees on sharp granite. We walked all through the night and into the dawn. I was constantly aware of the precious journal bound tightly to the small of my back, its edges chafing my skin. Once the sun was fully risen, our chaperones let us rest for an hour. Soon we were on our way again. I would not have believed we could walk for so long and in such grueling conditions, but fear is a powerful motivator.

By the second day, my sturdy boots were nothing but shreds. I bound them back together with rags and prayed they'd stay together. Then disaster struck. Aunt Besee slipped on an icy patch and twisted her knee.

She sat at the side of the road and crossed her arms. "I cannot go on," she said. "Please, Zeynep and Fatma, continue without me. I'll only hold you back."

She may be a small thing, but she is strong and wiry. I tried to pull her to her feet. She wouldn't budge.

"Please, Aunt Besee, we cannot leave you here."

Just then, a Dersim soldier approached us on a horse. It was Gurnaz. "You cannot stop here, Besee," he said. "It's not safe."

Aunt Besee looked up at him and scowled. "When I say it's impossible for me to walk any farther, I mean it."

Gurnaz dismounted and held out his hand. "Perhaps you cannot walk, but you can ride."

He gently got her to her feet, then lifted her with ease and set her on the back of his horse. In a graceful fluid movement, he got back up in front of her. "Wrap your arms around my waist, Besee," he said. "You're safe with me."

It took three days to reach the cold Euphrates River. The Turks had sunk all the barges, so the Dersim soldiers lashed together logs and we crossed precariously on these.

Much of what happened after that is an exhausted blur, but within days of the river crossing, our guides broke up the caravan and people went back to their own home villages in the mountains—except for those of us who had no home to return to.

Gurnaz took us to his own village and my heart ached when I caught my first glimpse of the snowy meadow hamlet through the trees: just a dozen or so well-constructed stone houses, some of which were two storeys tall.

He took us into his own house and introduced us to his daughter Maryam and grandson Seyit. I had met Seyit long ago when I worked at the hospital. He had accompanied his grandfather when Gurnaz came in with his foot swollen.

As I looked around the cozy cottage, I noticed a familiar carved walking staff propped up against the wall in one of the corners.

"When first we met," I said to Gurnaz, "You walked with that staff."

He smiled. "I'll never forget what a comfort it was to hear you speak Zaza."

Maryam loaned us fresh clothing and filled an enamel tub with warm water for bathing. It felt good to unbind the journal papers from my back. The pages were tinged with blood where they had dug into my skin.

We stayed with Maryam and Seyit for a number of weeks. Gurnaz came back from time to time, but mostly he was on patrol, guarding the Dersim communities from the Ottoman Army.

By summer, the Russians had broken through and we were able to cross over, but before we did, the village men returned for one evening and the dede held a semah for us all.

Ali, it was the first time in so long that I was able to perform the semah. Fatma and I were each paired with one of the Dersim soldiers and Besee danced with Gurnaz. As I closed my eyes and spun to the rhythm of the prayers, I imagined I danced with you.

Chapter Two

SS *Bergensfjord*, Norway

July 31, 1916

Dear Ali,

I am thousands of miles away from home, thousands of miles away from you, curled up inside a narrow wooden compartment in the crowded bottom level of a ship called the *Bergensfjord*. Suleyman rests his head against my knees and I am comforted by his presence, but the poor child has been sick. This isn't a serious illness like typhus, but something that afflicts anyone who is put in a small box inside a ship that sways on the sea. Were you sick too, my dear Ali, when you traveled to Canada?

Fatma is here as well, and her bed is above mine. Right now she is on the top deck with her head hanging over the side, throwing up. I would have stayed to comfort her, but it was more important to bring Suleyman down here where he can rest without the sound of his mother retching.

Aunt Besee is not with us. She decided to stay in the Dersim with Gurnaz. She says she feels at home there.

I am getting ahead of myself, but it's been so long since I've had a pen and paper that I could burst with all that I have to tell you. But first I must go back and check on Fatma.

Fatma is green with seasickness, but she's stopped vomiting and is now asleep. Suleyman is cuddled in with her and I'm sure they'll both feel better soon.

Now I must tell you how we've ended up on this ship. Norway is a neutral country and, despite the rain and mist, Bergen is a lively port. Many people from all over Europe and the Near East have arrived seeking refuge. For me, the most important thing is that Norway borders Russia, so we were able to get out.

The escapes through the Dersim began as a trickle, but for a very short period, thousands of Armenians got out safely through the mountains and over to Russia.

I gave Consul Davis' letter to the Russian authorities in Kars. And then we waited. War surrounded us, and in Russia, whispers of revolution. It was an unsettled and terrifying place to be, like Harput, but made worse as we didn't understand the Russian-speaking soldiers.

The ambassador arranged our safe passage north by train, truck, automobile, and horse all through the vast country. It wasn't until we stepped across the border into misty Norway that I began to feel safer. And I began to breathe easy once the *Bergensfjord* was out to sea. In the bottom deck we are surrounded by people jabbering away in Norwegian. I don't mind. It gives us privacy.

This solitude gives me time to translate the portions of my journal that have to do with the Armenian deportations. How I will get it to the proper authorities, I do not know, but Consul Davis told me I must. What I have witnessed is evidence of a terrible crime and the world must know about it, because, he says, that what we forget we are bound to repeat.

Chapter Three

BRANTFORD, ONTARIO

August 15, 1916

Dear Ali,

We went to 143 Darling Street, but a stranger answered.

I sat on a bench in Victoria Park, wondering what to do. Suleyman was beside me, exhausted and hungry, watching the pigeons while Fatma knocked on doors to find someone who knew where you or Yousef had gone.

Sometime later, she returned—with Hagop!

August 17, 1916

Dear Ali,

Hagop and Arsho have taken us in. It is a bittersweet time for all of us. I am thankful to know that you and Yousef are safe. Hagop told me about your arrest and imprisonment. I am heartsick to think of it.

But you are alive!

Six Armenians who got out through the Dersim came to Brantford in January, and so Hagop and Arsho heard firsthand about the killings. But they had no word about their own families in Eyolmez, and I had to break that terrible news. We are in mourning.

August 18, 1916

I showed Hagop my journal. He was overwhelmed with everything I had documented, but he understood its significance. He knows the mayor of Brantford and so he took me to the mayor's office today, with my journal. The mayor's secretary telephoned John Henry Fisher, the Member of Parliament for Brantford. Mr. Fisher came to Hagop's house in his automobile, took my journal and thanked me for my work. He said that he would ensure that the proper authorities get this. My journal was evidence of war crimes by the Young Turks against the Armenians, he said, and that it could be used in a court of law. I don't really understand any of this, but I do understand how important it is.

Chapter Four

NORTH OF TORONTO

August 21, 1916

As I look out the train window, I am grateful that I am alive. Suleyman sits across from me beside Fatma, and he looks at the pages of a colorful book—a present from Arsho. Fatma is pensive, staring out at nothing, and likely thinking of how she will break the news of their daughter's death to Yousef. How difficult it is to lose a child. How much more must it be to lose a child before you meet her? My heart aches for Yousef. This is the last letter I will write to you. Everything else I have to say to you will be face-to-face.

Love,

Zeynep

Chapter Five

KAPUSKASING, ONTARIO

August 21, 1916

When the train stopped, I opened my eyes. A station house with a sign that read "Kapuskasing." Could it really be true? Would I finally see Ali after all these years?

I stood up and stretched and tried to smooth the wrinkles out of my skirt. The stationmaster opened the door.

"Let me help you ladies down. I'll get your bags."

Fatma and Suleyman stepped off the train, then I followed. I tried to make sense of what was before me. The red-and-white station house seemed almost peaceful, but then I took a few steps to the left and looked beyond the tracks: two high barbed-wire fences patrolled by soldiers armed with bayonets.

A dirt road led up to the locked gate with a wooden sign: Kapuskasing Internment Camp. Two armed soldiers stood at attention.

This was where Ali had been kept all this time?

I looked beyond the gate: a huge parade ground flanked by rows of log buildings. Within the barbed-wire enclosure there were prisoners and soldiers doing chores.

There were hundreds of prisoners at the camp, but my eyes were drawn to one particular man. He wore faded overalls like all the rest and held a paintbrush in one hand. As he applied white paint to the broad wall of a building not far from the barbed wire, he favored his left leg. He had been hurt, that was clear.

It was Ali. I recognized the tilt of his head and the way that he frowned. I watched him methodically dip his brush into the paint can and carefully apply yet another stroke of white to the wall. It was as if the paint and the wall were his entire universe.

"Ali!" I cried. I dropped my handbag and ran toward the barbed-wire fence.

He didn't look up.

"Ali!"

He didn't seem to hear me. He dipped the paintbrush into the can once more.

I got to the first layer of the barbed wire and clutched it with my fingers. I shook the fence and shouted again, hot tears streaming down my cheeks.

"Ma'am, get away from the fence," said a soldier with a bayonet. I ignored him.

"Ali!" I shouted. I tried to climb up, but my dress got caught. Finally, Ali turned and his eyes met mine—the same eyes that I have loved all these years. They hadn't changed, even though his face was worn with worry.

Ali's face broke out into a huge smile. He threw the paintbrush down and limped toward me.

The soldier was practically upon me, his bayonet pointed in the air. "Ma'am, get away from the fence."

"Zeynep," said Ali, pushing his hand through the inner layer of barbed wire. "I love you so much!"

These were words that I had longed to hear. I reached my hand toward his. Two barbed-wire fences kept us apart. I reached through almost to my shoulder and Ali did the same, but we were still too far away from each other to touch.

"I am so sorry for leaving you," said Ali, pressing his face against the barbed wire.

"Don't be sorry," I told him. "Your last gift to me, the journal—it saved my life. And your mother's actions saved yours."

PART EIGHT

BRANTFORD, ONTARIO

December 1917

Mr. Brown called me over as the end-of-shift whistle blew. "I'm glad to have you back," he said. "The foundry wasn't the same without you."

"Thank you for putting in that request for my parole," I said. "My wife especially thanks you."

He smiled. "It was the least I could do."

I stepped out of the foundry and breathed the wintry air. It was good to be a free man once again and especially to have my old job back. Yes, I still had to report to the police station each week, but that was a small price to pay for my freedom. I walked down West Street past the train station and toward downtown, the same street I had marched through at the point of a bayonet long ago. But now, I wasn't a prisoner. Now I was a husband meeting my wife after work. I stepped into Angel's Confectionery. Zeynep was behind the counter, counting out gumdrops. At first she didn't notice me, but then she looked up and smiled.

"I'm almost finished," she said.

I sat on one of the stools by the soda fountain and watched Zeynep's delicate fingers as she sorted the candies into boxes. I could watch her all day.

The back door opened and Boulos Sarout stepped out. "Hello there, Ali. What a fine day this has been. Business is beginning to turn around." He turned to Zeynep. "I can finish that if you want to go home now," he said, grinning.

"Thank you. I'm just about done."

"Be on your way, then. I'll lock up. See you in the morning."

I helped Zeynep into her winter coat. As we walked toward home, I paused at the post office.

"This is the building that caused all your trouble," said Zeynep. "Bombing it, indeed."

"It's a beautiful building," I remarked. "There's something I've never shown you. Come here."

I clutched her hand and took her down an alleyway that opened up to a quiet courtyard behind the post office, almost completely enclosed by the backs of windowless buildings.

Zeynep stood in the middle of the open space and looked up at the early evening sky. "It's beautiful here."

"Brantford may not have mountains, but it has the sky and it has peace," I said. I took a deep breath. "Let's dance."

Zeynep faced me, smiling.

I stood with my arms at my side and looked up to the sky. Zeynep did the same. Together we sang one of our holy songs, just loud enough for us to get the rhythm. Then we raised our arms in unison and took the familiar steps. As we spun and danced, the memories of our lost loved ones joined us. Dancing the semah—with our family surrounding us in spirit—was pure joy.

We spun and danced for an hour or more, then stood there under the moon, clinging to each other and panting with exhaustion. The past, the present, the future: it was all here with us.

I kissed my wife on the lips and held her close.

"You are the other half of me."

AUTHOR'S NOTE

DANCE OF THE BANISHED is a work of fiction, but it is based on real historical events.

The idea for this novel sprouted five years ago when two Brantford historians, Wayne Hunter and William Darfler, showed me a stack of old newspaper clippings that recounted a series of events in the fall of 1914. Approximately 100 "enemy aliens" were rounded up in the middle of the night and put in the Brantford jail because of an unfounded rumor that they had attempted to blow up the local post office in an act of treason. Many of the men were ultimately sent to a World War I internment camp in Kapuskasing, Ontario. These men were victims of shameful wartime hysteria directed at foreigners, yet they had come to Canada because of its reputation for freedom and tolerance. Most of the 8,579 people interned were Ukrainian, but the 100 from Brantford were not.

That the incident happened in my hometown piqued my interest. As well, my grandfather had been interned at the same time for similar reasons, but he was imprisoned at a camp in

Jasper, Alberta. I knew the devastating effect internment had on my grandfather. What must it have been like for those 100 men from Brantford?

The men were identified as Turkish, but the same newspapers had described people like my Ukrainian grandfather as Austrian, so I knew to be skeptical. I dug deeper and found that although the men had come from Anatolia, which is now a part of modern-day Turkey, they were Kurdish, not Turkish. Adding more confusion to the mix, this particular group of Kurds was not Muslim, but Alevi, a 6,000-year-old religion that originated in Anatolia. Over the centuries Alevism has incorporated aspects of other religions. For example, Alevis consider Ali, the son-in-law of Muhammad, to be divine. Alevis avoid mosques and do not pray five times a day. And they consider women equal to men.

Some scholars believe that the Alevi Kurds of Anatolia are distantly related to the Armenians, who have also lived in Anatolia for thousands of years. There is an old saying: "The distance between Alevis and Armenians is no thicker than the membrane of an onion."

The key form of worship for Alevis is the semah, which is a nighttime twirling dance that men and women perform together without touching. The ritualized movement is said to reflect the rotation of the planets, and also Ali's ascension into heaven.

When the Alevis came to Brantford, they rented rooms from Armenians, who had been their friends and neighbors in

Anatolia, and who had come to Brantford a few years earlier.

As part of my research for Ali's story, I flew to Kapuskasing and walked the grounds of the former internment camp. I met with Julie Latimer, the curator at the Ron Morel Memorial Museum in Kapuskasing; and she showed me a wealth of photos, documents, and artifacts about the internment operations. One key document was a detailed diary written by one of the soldiers stationed at the camp.

To recreate the Brantford portion of Ali's story, those newspaper clippings were of tremendous help. I spent many hours at the Brantford Public Library, poring over microfilm copies of the *Brantford Expositor* and the *Courier* to read about day-to-day Brantford life a century ago. Isabel Kaprielian-Churchill's book, *Like Our Mountains: A History of Armenians in Canada*, was illuminating. I also accessed Isabel's dissertation from Archives Canada: "Sojourners from Keghi" (thesis); "Armenians in Ontario to 1915." I also read Isil Acehan's thesis, "Made in Massachusetts: Converting Hides and Skins Into Leather and Turkish Immigrants into Industrial Laborers (1860s-1920s)," as well as Frank Ahmed's *Turks in America*.

Zeynep's village life was inspired by a variety of sources, including century-old firsthand narratives written by western travelers who visited Anatolian villages. In order to recreate the day-to-day events in Harput during World War I and the Armenian Genocide, I had a wealth of eyewitness accounts, including diaries of missionaries and the writings of Consul Leslie Davis himself. For more general background on the Ottoman Empire during World War I, I read Hikmet Ozdemir's book, *The Otto-man Army 1914-1918*, which provided vivid documentation of just how deadly it was for regular soldiers. I also read *Ataturk* by Patrick Kinross, *Memoirs of Halidé Edib*, and numerous other books for a Turkish perspective of the era.

I have written five previous books set during the Arme-nian Genocide and so have amassed a significant collection of resources on that subject. But in all that writing and research, I completely missed an outstanding instance of bravery: the rescue of 40,000 Armenians by the Alevi Kurds of the Dersim Mountains. Once I knew what to look for, I went back through my collection and found references to this rescue operation in virtually all of the Harput eyewitness reports, but finding de-tailed accounts was a challenge. After much sleuthing, I was able to track down a couple of detailed first-person accounts by Armenians who were rescued through the Dersim Mountains.

The Alevi Kurds of the Dersim Mountains have been both rescuers and victims. In 1934, the Turkish government passed a law to assimilate minorities within Turkey, and thousands of Alevis were deported from the Dersim Mountains. They re-beled, and many thousands were massacred.

One last note, on my use of the term "Turkey." During World War I, the term was commonly used when referring to the Ottoman Empire, and so my characters do the same. The Republic of Turkey did not exist until 1923.

*Internees from the Ottoman Empire on a forced march;
Kapuskasing Internment Camp, circa 1915*

Internees stand for inspection; Kapuskasing Internment Camp, circa 1915

Internees flanked by armed guards; Kapuskasing Internment Camp, circa 1915

2015 Geoffrey Bilson Award

ACKNOWLEDGMENTS

MY SINCERE THANKS go to Suleyman Güven, who was born in the Dersim Mountains. Suleyman patiently answered all my questions and provided me with key information and cultural details. He translated material and read over an early draft of this manuscript for accuracy.

Thanks also to Jeff Burnham and his team at Goodminds, for sleuthing out Ellen Smallboy's wonderful book, *Glimpses of a Cree Woman's Life*. This detailed study was of tremendous help in recreating Nadie's world. As well, my appreciation goes to Gerald Chum of the Ininew Friendship Centre in Cochrane, Ontario, for reading my manuscript for accuracy. Thank you, Jim Etherington, the Kapuskasing Aboriginal Liaison, for connecting me with Gerald.

Sincere thanks to the great team at Pajama Press, including the publisher and my longtime mentor, Gail Winskill, who has believed in me since my first book, *Silver Threads*. Final and biggest thanks to my editor, Ann Featherstone, whose touch is light but oh so precise.